'Put it in. I'm ready.'

The sound that came from Kit's throat wasn't compliant, but he fed her without further comment. A dense, smooth and very cold cake melted on her tongue.

'Mmm, that one's powerful,' Sabrina said.

'Chocolate fondant cake. I thought we could make them in bite-size moulds so the guests can sample without feeling guilty.'

'Except that one bite isn't always enough.'

'Are you greedy?' He nudged against her thigh.

'No, but I am selfish,' she replied.

'What's the difference?'

'Greedy grabs. Selfish…savours.' Sabrina moved her leg into the pressure, rocking her hips. 'I want to savour *you*,' she said.

'I've been here for the taking.'

She was ready to sample every inch of Kit in bite-size gulps. Delaying had only made her more ravenous.

'Your chin is covered in chocolate dust.' He swiped at it with his thumb. She heard a smacking sound. 'Umm. You taste good.'

'A kiss would taste even better,' she purred.

Dear Reader,

Survey says: 50% of women prefer chocolate to sex.

The reasoning is that when women eat chocolate they experience the same pleasures in their brain as being in love. As a writer, when I read that I immediately cooked up a story. If a woman was trying to give up men, would chocolate cure her craving? What type of man would most tempt her?

Sisters Sabrina and Mackenzie Bliss have made a bet to change their lives—with a diamond ring at stake. In the first book of the SEX & CANDY duo, pastry chef Kit Rex convinces Sabrina to indulge...in chocolate, in pleasure and in romance. Be sure to look for Mackenzie's story, *Sinfully Sweet*, available next month.

Please visit my website at www.carriealexander.com for fun facts, a candy contest, Kit's recipes and a chocolate personality quiz. I'd love to hear from you!

Carrie Alexander

Available next month
Sinfully Sweet by Carrie Alexander

THE CHOCOLATE SEDUCTION

by

Carrie Alexander

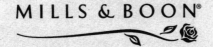

MILLS & BOON®

To the Aztec and Mayan discoverers of the cacao
bean: all your fault!

*First published in Great Britain 2004
by Harlequin Mills & Boon Limited,
Eton House, 18-24 Paradise Road, Richmond, Surrey TW9 1SR*

© Carrie Antilla 2003

ISBN 0 263 83993 1

21-0104

*Printed and bound in Spain
by Litografia Rosés S.A., Barcelona*

Prologue

"SOME WEDDING," Sabrina Bliss said to her sister. "I nearly lost it when the minister got to the 'till death do us part' part." Mackenzie would understand what she meant.

"That's why I pinched you!" Mackenzie tried to put on a scolding face, but warm laughter bubbled up instead. "It's *so* rude to laugh in the middle of a wedding ceremony."

Sabrina smiled, feeling oddly light and cheerful despite her doubts about the marriage. "You'll notice I didn't object, either."

Mackenzie blinked. "Do you have objections?"

"Mmm...no, not really."

"But you're not optimistic."

Sabrina tucked her fist beneath her chin, fingers tightening around the small velvet box in her palm. She should give it up, but...she just wasn't sure about letting go.

"You know I don't believe in fairy-tale endings," she said.

Sabrina and Mackenzie had come out onto the balcony of the Fontaine Hotel to catch a quiet moment together, away from the reception. They'd found their newlywed parents, Charlie and Nicole Bliss, dancing beneath the starry sky on one of the brick paths of the hotel's rose garden. Light and music spilled from the open French doors, dappling the scene with a particularly picturesque version of romance.

Bah, humbug, Sabrina thought, without much conviction. Her emotions were too close to the surface. Luckily she had plenty of experience in not letting them show.

Mackenzie was the opposite. And clearly a goner. She'd welled up throughout the ceremony, and now her gaze was pinned on their parents, her big dark eyes shining with hope.

A couple of months ago, Charlie and Nicole Bliss had confessed to their daughters that they'd never quite managed to fall out of love despite their divorce of long standing. They'd decided to give marriage another try. Sabrina and Mackenzie had been stunned. Aside from the occasional family Christmas dinner or birthday party, they hadn't known that their parents were seeing each other. Naturally, Mackenzie found it all so touching and romantic. Sabrina wasn't as ready to forget the perils of the rancorous divorce, even though it had taken place sixteen years ago, when she was thirteen. And she sure didn't want to be around if the shrapnel started to fly again.

"Maybe it's not a fairy-tale ending," Mackenzie said softly. "Maybe it's real."

"Ha." Sabrina raised a champagne glass to her lips. "When reality hits, I give them six months."

Mackenzie wrapped a hand around her sister's arm. She squeezed, making Sabrina wish she could take back her words. Mackenzie was a squeezer, a patter, a cheerer-upper. And a very good friend. They'd been apart for too long. Mackenzie was settled in New York City while Sabrina went wherever whim took her.

"You're so cynical, Breen," she said, reverting to the family nickname.

Did that mean they were a family again?

Sabrina shrugged. While she might have her doubts about her parents, Mackenzie was as reliable as a rock. The sisters had very different personalities, but they'd turned to each other for comfort after the divorce and had been close ever since, even when separated by thousands of miles.

"Look at the divorce statistics," Mackenzie continued. "If half of all marriages fail, then Mom and Dad already have their divorce over and done with. This marriage is practically a sure thing."

Sabrina scoffed. "Your numbers are skewed. I'd definitely double down on that bet." She'd learned the lingo in Reno, where she'd once worked as a cocktail waitress after a stage magician had fired her for screaming bloody murder during a botched saw trick. "Here I thought logic was your strong suit."

"This isn't about logic. You've got to have faith."

"*Faith?* How?"

Mackenzie gazed past the balcony to their parents. "Look at them. Tell me your heart doesn't melt."

Sabrina held the ring box in one hand and sipped champagne from the glass in the other, brooding over the sight of her parents exchanging whispers and kisses after all these years. They were a study in contrasts, much like their daughters. Charlie Bliss was tall and sandy-haired, prone to daydreaming and wild, irresponsible schemes. Nicole was as short, round and stable as Mackenzie, but not as gentle. She could be a bulldozer.

Sabrina truly wished them the best. But whatever

faith she had had been left behind years ago, dug deep into the bottom of the backpack she'd lugged between their houses after the divorce.

Six months was generous, she decided. It wouldn't be too much of a shock if they were arguing on the honeymoon cruise, when Charlie wanted to go parasailing and Nicole chose to snorkel. Every little thing had once been a battle. The arguments were still familiar.

"Sure, they seem devoted," Sabrina admitted. A spring breeze whipped up and stole the words *"for now..."* from her lips. Loose pink rose petals from the swags draped over the balcony railing scattered like confetti. Cream satin ribbons fluttered.

Below, Nicole's delighted laughter rang out as Charlie removed the jacket of his tux and draped it over her shoulders. He used it to pull her toward his kiss.

Mackenzie sighed. "See that?"

Sabrina nodded, watching. Even *her* heart had melted...a little. Then the wind came again and she shivered in her whisper-of-silk slip dress. Ever practical and prepared, Mackenzie hooked an arm around Sabrina's shoulders, sharing her pink cashmere wrap and her body warmth. Mackenzie was a home-and-hearth kind of girl. Sabrina was long and lean, built for running.

She was good at that. But then why was she still clutching the ring box so tightly?

Mackenzie stirred. "Doesn't it make you think, Breen?"

"Think what?"

"Mom and Dad aren't afraid to go for it. We shouldn't be, either."

Sabrina drew away. "What are you talking about? Love? Marriage? *Me?* Not on your life!"

Making a tutting noise, Mackenzie pulled off the wrap and arranged it around her sister. Her long hair covered her own shoulders like a cape. It was beautiful—waist-length, thick and wavy, the color of dark chocolate. She'd been wearing it in the same plain style since she was ten. "No, Sabrina. I mean change. Transformation, renewal, starting over—whatever you want to call it. Change would do us both good."

Sabrina made a face. "It's my policy to avoid anything that will do me good. And I like my life the way it is."

Mackenzie's brows went up. "Do you really?"

"Yes, really."

"I remember a certain 3:00 a.m. phone call—"

"You swore you wouldn't use that against me. It was no more than a bad breakup rant. I'd already done the sympathy margarita thing with my girlfriends. I was in the middle of the tearing-up-photos-and-freaking-long-distance stage."

"Now, Sabrina, you were with the last guy for almost an entire winter. It was more than just another failed relationship. You're used to those. If you weren't hurt, you wouldn't have packed up and flown to Mexico the very next day."

"I'm used to doing that, too," Sabrina pointed out.

Mackenzie got a stubborn look on her face. "Just because you're used to it doesn't mean you like it. I distinctly remember that before the breakup you were wondering if it wasn't time to settle down and start a real career."

Sabrina hesitated. Mackenzie was right. Lately she'd

been nagged by the feeling that she'd been a gypsy for long enough—continually moving from city to city, job to job, one boyfriend to the next. All that had gotten her was a lot of experience, an address book full of crossed-out names and a Mr. Wrong in nearly every state.

She *was* ready for a change—a smart one, this time.

"What about you?" she challenged Mackenzie. "I know you're the good sister and all, but there's room for improvement in your life, too. How long have you been in a holding pattern with Mr. Dull? And hasn't your boss at Regal Foods been promising you a promotion to executive in charge of jawbreakers and Gummi Bears for, I don't know, forever and a day?"

Mackenzie's mouth pursed. "You haven't been keeping up. I was promoted nearly a month ago, when you were jet-skiing in Mazatlan."

"Uh, wow. That's fabulous. Congrats, and all that." Sabrina wondered how her sister stood it, being so steady and reliable all the time. She really ought to offer the family's heirloom ring to Mackenzie, except that...

"And how is Mr. Dull?" Sabrina asked.

"His name is Jason Dole. He's—"

"A deep snooze. A dead bore."

"You're wrong. He might not be up to your Danger Boy standards, but he's a good guy."

Sabrina rolled her eyes. "There's that word again. *Good.* The kiss of death."

"Not for me. We're alike. We get along."

"You wouldn't be talking change if all you wanted was to 'get along.'" Ever since the divorce had turned their world upside down, Mackenzie had been resistant to change. She'd lived in the same apartment since college, worked at the same candy company as she slowly worked her way toward a position as the top Tootsie Roll. She had to be as tired of routine as Sabrina was of airports and train stations.

"Look," she said, nudging Mackenzie toward the railing again. Charlie and Nicole had continued to kiss. Aside from the slight *ew* factor—this was their middle-aged parents, after all—the couple's affection was enviable. "Tell me you have that much passion with Jason and I'll gladly dance at your wedding." *And even surrender the ring.*

"I can't." The admission came too fast. Mackenzie wasn't nearly as resistant as Sabrina had expected.

"Well, then, there you go." Sabrina cocked her head. Charlie and Nicole were *still* kissing. She leaned over the railing and yelled, "Hey! You kids down there. Getta room, why don'tcha?"

Her parents broke apart, looking around in surprise. When they spotted their daughters up on the balcony, they laughed and waved, calling hellos.

Sabrina lifted her glass to them, then drained the remaining champagne in one swallow. "Mackenzie— I've got it. You and I need to switch lives."

"Oh, no. I'm not cut out for changing boyfriends with the seasons. And I can't roller-skate." Sabrina's latest temporary job was as a roller-skating waitress in a fifties-theme drive-in restaurant in St. Louis, a city she'd chosen by poking her finger at a map in a travel agency's window.

"But we do need to make changes," Mackenzie went on. She took a breath. Stuck out her chin. "I will if you will."

Sabrina narrowed her eyes. "What did you have in

mind?" It wasn't like her sister to be reckless, so *she* was forced to be cautious in response. One way or another, they always balanced each other out.

"For your part, you'll settle down in one city. Sign a real lease, not a month-by-month."

That wasn't so bad. "You have to break up with Mr. Dull."

Mackenzie nodded. "I can do that. If you get a job— a job you like enough to stick with for at least a year."

"An entire year..." Sabrina gulped, then leveled a finger at Mackenzie's round face. "Fine, but *you* have to quit the candy company."

"Quit Regal Foods? Why? I told you how I just got that big promotion."

"You've always talked about running your own fancy candy store. I know you've been saving for it. Why not crack open your nest egg? There's no better time to go for it."

Mackenzie had paled, but she nodded. Reluctantly. "I'll take the plunge if you promise to give up men," she said, probably because she'd calculated that it was a safe offer which would never be accepted.

Celibacy? Sabrina thought. That was absurd! Impossible! But she retaliated without voicing her doubts. "Only if you cut your hair."

"How short?"

"How long?" Sabrina said at the same time.

"Until you *truly* fall in love," Mackenzie answered.

Sabrina's fingers clenched on the ring box. "Then you go above the ears."

The sisters stopped, momentarily dumbstruck by their careening conversation.

"My hair?" Mackenzie whispered, lifting a hand to stroke the dark length of it.

"No men?" Sabrina said, her voice faint and very far away. She couldn't possibly. She loved men. She was addicted to testosterone.

Mackenzie's eyes sharpened. "One year to change our lives. I say we shake on it!" And bam, she stuck out her hand without taking the usual week to think over the decision.

Sabrina wavered. "I..."

"Chicken?"

"Of course not. But what are the stakes?"

"The journey is its own reward."

"Phooey. How about this?" Sabrina flung back the cashmere wrap and held out her hand, palm up.

Mackenzie froze, staring at the worn blue velvet box which was familiar to both of them. Finally she reached out to flip up the lid and reveal the diamond ring that Nicole Bliss had removed from her finger the day of her divorce and stuck way in the back of her jewel box, saying she never wanted to see it again. Now and then, when their mother wasn't home, the sisters had sneaked in to take the ring out and try it on. Sabrina had wanted to believe that her attachment to the ring was the usual girlish attraction to shiny jewelry, but now that it was hers, she knew it meant more than that. Romance, love, marriage—which she wasn't supposed to believe in.

"Grandmother's diamond solitaire?" Mackenzie said, awed.

"Mom gave it to me before the ceremony." Charlie had presented Nicole with a new ring to symbolize their fresh start, so she'd passed the heirloom on to her oldest daughter.

"But I'm not sure I want it," Sabrina added hurriedly. "You'll be getting married before me. I mean, I have no intention of ever getting—"

"No, no, you're the oldest." Mackenzie gazed longingly at the ring. "You should have it."

"Ugh, I knew you'd be noble. That's why I want to put it up as the prize in our bet. The one of us who most successfully changes her life in the next year gets to keep the ring. We'll make the decision on our parent's first anniversary—if they last that long."

Mackenzie laughed in disbelief. "That's so—so—"

"Sacrilegious? It's only a ring." Sabrina slapped the velvet box into Mackenzie's palm, then impulsively tossed the champagne flute over the railing. "I'm not giving you time to change your mind. We have a deal!" They shook hands, clasping them around the treasured ring box. The sound of glass shattering on the patio below seemed appropriate. They were breaking out, starting off new. Just like—

Well, maybe not *just* like their parents, Sabrina thought when she glanced over the balcony. Charlie was laughing and Nicole was pulling out of his embrace, trying to get away so she could stalk over to the balcony and scold Sabrina for being so careless.

Typical.

But even as Sabrina watched, Charlie managed to grab hold of his wife's hand. He kissed Nicole on the cheek, placating her with a few murmured words, then raised a fist, shaking it playfully at his daughters. "Which one broke the glass?" he called. "A shard might have flown up and nicked my beautiful bride's face.''

Sabrina and Mackenzie looked at each other and grinned. ''Sorry,'' they sang in unison, standing shoulder to shoulder.

There was no good reason for it, especially with grown-up responsibility and a crazy celibacy promise looming in her future, but Sabrina's spirits soared when she looked into her parents' upturned faces. Charlie was balding and Nicole had lost the battle of the bulge. They had wrinkles and graying hair and fallen arches. There had been sieges when they'd threatened that widowhood was an even better solution than divorce, yet here they were, holding on to each other, trying again, their timeworn faces glowing with love. What courage they had.

Maybe, Sabrina thought, recognizing that the tiny part of herself that still believed in love wasn't buried as deep as she'd thought. *Maybe this time....*

1

Six weeks later

FLEXING MUSCLES and swirling chocolate—Sabrina Bliss was in heaven. *I could get used to this,* she told herself, immensely pleased to have found an aspect of her new job that would still be fun a year from now...if she stayed with it that long.

And she might if this kept up, even without an heirloom engagement ring at stake. How lucky could one woman get?

The sight of male muscles bulging and rippling over pots of melting chocolate or whizzing mixers was an everyday occurrence at Decadence. In her first week as lunch manager, she'd learned to time her breaks to catch ten minutes of the show as Kristoffer "Call me Kit" Rex concocted the day's desserts. The renowned pastry chef almost always featured chocolate, his specialty.

Today Kit was working with semisweet chocolate, coconut and phyllo triangles. Sheets of the paper-thin pastry were stacked nearby under a dampened kitchen towel. He removed the cover of the food processor he'd used to chop the high-quality French chocolate he insisted on even though it took a big bite out of the restaurant's dessert budget. He added softened butter and the toasted coconut to the mixture.

"Please pass me the knife." The request didn't register with Sabrina for a second or two because she was distracted with comparing Kit's rich voice to an image of warm chocolate pouring over his naked body.

When she didn't react, he reached for the knife, his bare arm brushing against hers. Skin on skin, the contact was as sharp and sensual as a swallow of chocolate-laced amaretto cream. She could gain weight merely listening to him. Actual touching brought her one chocolate kiss away from orgasm.

I shouldn't be here, she reminded herself, thinking of her pact with Mackenzie. *The temptation is too much.*

Kit's knife was a blur as he chopped almonds in five seconds flat. He scraped them into the food processor, his biceps bulging as he lifted the hefty chopping board.

Yum. Sabrina tried to smack her lips, but her tongue was parched. Probably from all the panting.

Kit replaced the lid and blended the chocolate with the other ingredients, shooting a sexy little grin at his audience of one. She grinned back at him, not even trying to hide her interest. Let him think she was a wanna-be chef or a slavering chocoholic. Anything but what she was—a sex-starved celibate who was ready to crawl inside his starched white chef's coat and eat him whole.

He moved over a step and stirred a saucepan of melting butter on the stove. She used the inside of her loose V-neck tank to blot the dampness on her chest. The kitchen was always hot, but even if they were in an igloo, watching Kit cook would make her sweat.

At five-eleven, he was only an inch or so taller than Sabrina, but his nicely developed chest, arms and thighs more than made up for the slight lack of height. He had black hair that was one week's growth away from shaggy, penetrating blue eyes and the kind of hollow cheeks and strong jaw that looked best shadowed with stubble.

Fortunately for Manhattan's female population, his stubble usually complied.

Sabrina fanned herself. Oh, yeah, the man was hot. The gold ring that pierced his left ear gave him the look of a pirate. Even his eyelids were sexy—drooping slightly whenever he lapsed into a moment of silent brooding. He didn't talk a lot when he cooked—or any other time, for that matter—but he was quick with a smile or a joke. He cared about people. She'd seen him quietly inquiring after the dishwasher's college applications and the vegetable delivery guy's daughter who had tonsillitis.

Kristoffer Rex had fascinated Sabrina ever since her first day on the job at Decadence, a Manhattan restaurant that was a major step up from serving burgers on roller blades. Not a single member of the kitchen crew or serving staff had a bad word to say about him, but none of them knew his story either. She'd asked outright—asked everyone but Kit. The essence of himself, who he was, where he'd come from and how he lived outside of the restaurant, had been kept strictly private. To learn more, she'd have to get closer to the actual man.

And that, given her bet with Mackenzie, was simply not going to happen.

Sabrina gave a silent, inward groan. She'd have to content herself with watching Kit make his chocolate desserts. Even if that raised her body temperature to the boiling point.

A strip of the phyllo dough had been laid out on the work surface. He brushed melted butter across it, then looked over at Sabrina. "Want to help?" Practically the first words he'd spoken to her, other than "Taste this," or "Good morning."

She caught her tongue between her teeth, then nodded. "Sure."

"Come over here beside me."

She pushed off the stool and went to stand next to him. He smelled like bittersweet chocolate, darkly sweet and delicious. *Gobble, gobble, slurp,* she thought, humming with vibrations at his nearness.

"You can be the folder." Kit put a heaping spoonful of his chocolate mixture onto a corner of the pastry strip. He showed her how to fold the corner into a triangle, then again onto itself, continuing along the entire strip until the filling was wrapped in the airy layers of phyllo dough.

"Not bad," Sabrina said as she transferred the pastry puff onto a baking sheet.

"You're a natural, kid."

She looked into his amused eyes. They gave her a charge, even though she could see that he was humoring her. The other chefs tended be high-strung and easily annoyed, so she'd learned to stay out of their way. But the pastry chef's work station was set off to one side, and Kit didn't seem to mind when she hung around.

Still...

Kid, huh?

It had been a long time since an attractive man

looked at her as a kid sister. She didn't like it. True, she had no intentions of hooking up with Kit. Nevertheless it didn't seem right for him to dismiss the possibility so easily.

"Fold," he said, and she realized he'd laid out another strip of the delicate dough and spooned out a dollop of chocolate. They worked together in silence for a few minutes until the first pan was filled with neat rows of the triangles. Now and then, their elbows bumped or their hands brushed and Sabrina got more and more peeved that Kit had no reaction at all when *she* was struggling not to make cheesy analogies about oozing filling and hot home cookin'.

One of the servers, Charmaine Piasceki, stepped through the stainless-steel swinging doors that led out to the dining room. "Sabrina, your sister's here." She looked at Sabrina's buttery fingers, then over at Kit. "Should I tell her you're greased up with one of the chefs?"

Out of Kit's range, Sabrina made a menacing face at Charmaine, who'd become a friend as soon as they realized they both had smart mouths, food tattoos and opposite tastes in men. Despite kooky pink hair and a Persephone's pomegranate on the small of her back, Charmaine went for uptight lawyers and investment bankers. She liked to turn them on to their wild side.

Sabrina wiped her fingers on the towel keeping the phyllo dough pliable. "I'll be there as soon as we're finished with the filling."

Charmaine pushed backward through the doors with her rump. She looked at Kit and laughed, flashing the silver stud in her tongue. "Sure thing. We wouldn't want you two to skimp on the filling."

Sabrina's gaze skidded across Kit's face. He was grinning at her again. She gulped, too aware of the heat flushing her cheeks. "Umm. Well, that was fun, but I have to get back out there."

"I'll bring you and your sister a sample, fresh from the oven. Well-filled."

"Great." She meant it. Maybe if Mackenzie saw Kit in the flesh—the living, breathing, warm, rippling flesh—she'd let Sabrina out of the "no men" part of their deal. Mackenzie was reasonable. She'd understand that there was only so much she could expect her sister to resist.

The quiet, clean public area of the restaurant was a relief after the hot zone of the kitchen. Sabrina stopped at the bar and got a couple of bottled waters from a small fridge. She uncapped one of them and took a long swig of the icy liquid to soothe her parched throat as she surveyed the activity in the front room. Servers moved from table to table in their stark white-and-black uniforms, doing the final prep work before they opened for the lunch trade.

Mackenzie had been seated at a table by one of the windows that overlooked West Broadway. The prime Tribeca location went hand in hand with the restaurant's gourmet menu, hip reputation and a parade of well-heeled patrons who liked to rub shoulders with the funkier creative types. Word was that although a real working artist might actually starve on the minuscule portions served at Decadence, they could never afford them.

"Hey, sis." Sabrina set the blue bottles on the table and slid into one of the Danish modern chairs. "What happened? Your hair's still long." She'd made an appointment for Mackenzie at a Madison Avenue salon recommended by one of the restaurant's owners, the famously stylish Dominique Para.

Mackenzie looked up, guilt written across her face. "I'm sorry. I backed out at the last minute."

"No! Do you know I had to give Dominique my favorite flea-market boots as a bribe for your appointment? I won't mention how hard it is to find authentic Victorian lace-ups in my size." Sabrina's feet were long and thin, like the rest of her. Dominique, a former model, was a perfect match, size-wise.

"I just couldn't go through with it," Mackenzie said, blinking puppy-dog eyes.

"Do I have to go with you to hold your hand?"

"Yes, please."

Sabrina wagged her head. "What's the hang-up with your hair? You've managed everything else. You quit your job, the new candy store is opening on schedule, Mr. Dull has been given his walking papers..." She caught Mackenzie's blank look. "He *is* gone, isn't he?"

"More or less. It's not my fault that he keeps sending flowers."

Sabrina flipped a hand. "Jason has no imagination. He wants you back because you're easy."

"Ah, no, I think that would be you." One side of Mackenzie's mouth curled into a dimple as she twisted off the cap of her water.

"Touché. But you know I meant easy as in comfortable." Sabrina moved restlessly in her chair, flinging one arm over the molded bird's-eye maple backrest and tossing her hair over the other shoulder. "I'm not easy any longer, you know. And, man, is it killing me."

Mackenzie was busy looking around the restaurant.

Decadence was as polished and chic as Dominique Para herself, filled with a striking combination of mid-century design and trendy art-house accessories. Partial walls made of woven maple planks separated certain areas for privacy. Sculptural sheet-glass mobiles doubled as lighting. Swivel chairs in purple and acid-green, paired with steel ashtray pedestals from the '50s, made the wait in the lounge for a table more of a pleasure than a bother. At first, Sabrina hadn't been sure that she fit in at Decadence with a wardrobe that was primarily made up of jeans, sweats, tanks and bandannas, but Dominique had passed along a selection of designer dresses that were so perfectly simple and well-fitted they had to be couture.

Mackenzie returned her attention to her sister. "I thought the restaurant would be keeping you so busy you wouldn't have time to think about men."

"That would be the goal," Sabrina said, "except I haven't told you about Kit Rex yet."

"Kit Rex? Isn't he a rock star?"

"Not Kid Rock," Sabrina started to explain, before she saw that Mackenzie was teasing.

"Super. There *would* have to be a man in the picture." Mackenzie affected a put-upon sigh. "Okay. How bad do you have it?"

Sabrina fanned her face. "Very, very bad."

Mackenzie didn't speak for a long minute. Sabrina could see the cogs grinding beneath the mass of pinned-up hair. Her sister had a solution for every problem, if she was given enough time to think it over.

Mackenzie's eyes slitted. Sabrina shifted under the scrutiny, examining her manicure, then flicking a dot of chocolate filling off the front of her hand-me-down dress. It was lilac, sleeveless, A-line—very Jackie O.

Finally Mackenzie lifted a finger. "Chocolate," she announced.

"Chocolate? Chocolate is what's getting me into this predicament."

"I don't understand."

Sabrina leaned over the table, lowering her voice. "Kit is our head pastry chef. He specializes in chocolate desserts. Several times a day, I'm drawn into the kitchen by the force of his sheer animal magnetism to watch him work. He's...well...he's charming on the surface, but kind of quiet and deep underneath. He's got major sex appeal without trying at all. I'm having fantasies about tying him up in apron strings and driz- zling chocolate over his naked chest." Sabrina stopped and sucked in a breath to steady herself. "So trust me, chocolate is *not* the answer."

Mackenzie snapped her mouth shut. "Wow." She glanced around the restaurant, probably looking for Kit. "I haven't seen you this worked up in a long time."

Sabrina had the answer to that. Normally she wasn't overly introspective, but she'd had nothing to do for the past seven sleepless nights except think. "That's be- cause I usually satisfy my cravings as they come. I've never had to do this denial thing before. Turns out my willpower is flabby from lack of use." She put her chin in her hand, ruing the day they'd made the bet. If the ring wasn't at stake, and if she didn't have this odd emotional attachment to it despite her negativity to- ward marriage...

"But you haven't given in," Mackenzie said with some doubt.

"Not yet. Hell, I'm not even sure that Kit is interested."

Mackenzie laughed. "Right. Like I believe that."

"Why wouldn't you?"

"Has there ever been a guy who didn't want you? You're the average American male's dream girl. Tall, pretty, long legs, blond hair…"

"But no va-va-voom." Sabrina motioned to her small breasts. "Maybe Kit is a boob man."

Mackenzie giggled. "They're all boob men. Fortunately, a woman needs only a pair of boobs to satisfy that requirement. Any size will do."

"Doesn't matter. Kit doesn't seem like a T&A hound. Or if he is, he's subtle about it."

"Gay?"

"No way." Half the chefs were, but not Kit.

"Maybe he senses your determination to remain celibate and he respects the decision."

"Yeah, but the thing is…I'm not that determined."

"You promised, Breen."

"Don't pull that Breen stuff. You got me at Mom and Dad's wedding while I was momentarily overcome by sentiment. It's not going to work again."

"Doesn't matter," Mackenzie said in her placid, content way. "The deal's still in force."

"Yeah, but—"

"No buts."

"You haven't met Kit. He's a very big *but*." Sabrina held up a hand. "Don't laugh. As long as your hair hasn't been cut—"

"Next week—no, tomorrow. I'll get it cut tomorrow."

"—I'm within my rights to renege. If Kit so much as

wiggles a finger at me, I'm going to be naked and climbing all over him while the dishwashers applaud."

"Good." Mackenzie grinned. "I've always dreamed of getting grandmother's ring."

"Not so fast. I may be weak, but I'm still holding out." Sabrina crossed her fingers beneath her chin in hopes that she could continue.

"Only another ten months or so to go," Mackenzie said airily. "Remember, you have to last until Mom and Dad's first anniversary."

"You mean their *second* first anniversary." Sabrina snorted. "Of course, you're going to lose long before that if you don't get your hair cut and send Mr. Dull to Decadence to meet Charmaine."

Mackenzie hooted. "Wait a minute! What's that about Charmaine?"

"Jason's just her type. After she loosens his tie and gets him into a pair of leather pants, he'll never bother you again. Unless you'd rather keep him than win the bet?"

"Sure, let Charmaine at him." Mackenzie gave a careless wave. "You overplayed your hand. He was never my dream man."

Sabrina's thoughts immediately veered to Kit. She squirmed. "Oh, God, what have I done? I'll never hold out for another month, let alone ten of them. I'm not sure I can do another *day*."

Mackenzie cocked her head. Her lips had compressed into a smug little smile. "You can if we dose you up with chocolate."

Sabrina was baffled. "All the better. I'll apply the chocolate and he can lick it off me."

"You miss my point. The chocolate will be a *substitute* for sex."

Sabrina gaped, but before she could question the preposterous statement, she caught a glimpse of Kit, crossing the dining room. He carried two plates.

"Welcome to my torture," she whispered to Mackenzie right before he arrived.

"Mademoiselles." Kit bobbed his head so a curl of jet-black hair fell across his forehead. He set the dessert plates before them, his blue eyes twinkling.

Sabrina had to look away. She stared at the plate. The phyllo triangle had been baked golden brown, set in a pool of raspberry puree and drizzled with a spiderweb of dark chocolate syrup. A dollop of rich vanilla ice cream and a ripe red raspberry nestled beside it.

Too much temptation for one weak woman to withstand. She said in a low voice, "Mackenzie, this is Kristoffer Rex."

Mackenzie was gazing up at him without blinking. "I figured."

"Call me Kit," he said.

"Kit, I'd like you to meet Mackenzie Bliss, my sister."

Mackenzie's smile was a little too wide and far too dazzled. "Nice to meet you." She offered her hand.

Kit took it. "My pleasure."

"Oh, no, the pleasure's all mine." Mackenzie raised her eyebrows at Sabrina, then glanced at her plate. "This looks scrumptious."

"Phyllo with coconut, almond and chocolate filling. Please taste it before the ice cream melts."

Mackenzie opened the chartreuse napkin folded around her utensils. "Won't you join us?"

Sabrina's stomach flip-flopped. "He can't, he's preparing—"

"Love to," Kit said. "For a minute." He glanced at Sabrina for approval before pulling a chair out.

She nodded, edging her chair over an inch. The kidney-shaped table shrank to half its previous size. "We should both get back to work."

"You have time to test my dish. That's work, isn't it?" Kit's eyes crinkled...at Mackenzie.

Sabrina stabbed the pastry and the warm chocolate filling oozed out. Mackenzie took a bite and rolled her eyes skyward. "Mmm, delicious."

Kit smiled a thank-you and then looked at Sabrina. "What do you think, boss?"

She lifted a bit of the flaky pastry to her lips, wondering what had happened to *kid*. Kit knew she wasn't his boss, of course. She was in charge of the serving staff and the lunch receipts and reported to the restaurant's head manager each evening. The owners, Dominique and her partner, Curt Tyrone, dropped in occasionally, greeting guests and standing around gossiping while showing off their fabulous selves to best advantage.

"Very good," Sabrina said. "Although I don't have much of a sweet tooth."

Kit lounged in his chair, fingers laced over his abdomen. "Oh?"

"It's true," Mackenzie put in earnestly. "Sabrina's taste buds are geared toward spicy foods. But I was just telling her that she should start eating more chocolate."

Sabrina would have kicked her sister under the table, but Kit's stretched-out legs were in the way. He wore faded jeans and battered running shoes under his double-breasted chef's coat.

"We should all make it a habit to eat a bit of chocolate every day," Kit said. "It does a body good."

"Exactly," Mackenzie said. "But Sabrina only likes what's bad for her."

"Ha." Sabrina licked ice cream off her spoon. "My sister's in the candy business," she told Kit.

"How interesting." He focused on Mackenzie. "What do you do?"

"I worked at Regal Foods in the sweets division until recently. Now I'm opening my own penny-candy emporium in the Village. It's to be called Sweet Something." Mackenzie shot her sister a mischievous glance. "Sabrina will have to bring you to the grand opening."

Kit's gaze slid sideways; Sabrina felt it slip over her like warm honey. "I'd be delighted."

She stabbed the phyllo. "That's marvy. So would I."

"Then it's a date," Mackenzie said.

Sabrina glared. She was going to take the scissors to her sister's hair herself and she would be no gentler than when she'd shorn all their Barbie dolls and made Mackenzie cry.

Mackenzie went on as if Sabrina wasn't giving her the squinty-eyed death ray. "What about you, Kit? How did you come to work at Decadence?"

He shrugged. "Curt and Dominique found me working at a resort in Tahiti. They liked my desserts and offered me a job. I've never lived in New York City, so I gave it a try."

"Do you move around a lot?"

"I have."

"So does Sabrina. You two must have a lot in common."

Again, Sabrina felt Kit's eyes on her, but this time they weren't nearly as warm. "Is that so?"

"I like change." She put down her spoon, realizing she'd polished her plate without being aware of it. The sweetness of the dessert lingered on her tongue, and she rather liked it. The rich chocolate was giving her a glow inside.

An awkward silence had fallen, so Mackenzie moved the conversation forward in her usual faciliatory way. "Where are you from, Kit?"

"A small town in Ohio. But I've lived all over."

"You have the slightest accent. It doesn't sound like Ohio to me."

"I'm homogenized. A little Midwest twang, a little New England, a little French and Italian, all mixed up with a teaspoon of the lazy island lilt."

Mackenzie was getting more out of him in five minutes than Sabrina had in a week. But then, very little of their time together had been spent talking. Just staring, at least for her part. "Mackenzie and I grew up in suburban New York."

"Scarsdale." Mackenzie nodded. "Our parents are still there."

"What do you mean *still?*" Sabrina said, even though Kit was watching and listening.

"Again, then." Mackenzie explained for Kit's benefit. "Mom and Dad divorced when I was twelve and Sabrina was thirteen. They remarried six weeks ago."

Sabrina rolled her eyes. "It's a suburban American fairy tale."

"Sounds like it to me." Kit stood and took their plates. "I have to go back to work."

"Too late," Sabrina said, giving him a saucy chin tilt and a flick of her hair. "You've already been reported to management."

Kit bent closer. "Then *management* will have to punish me."

She was riveted by his eyes. "Fifty lashes with a limp cannoli."

"Kinky," he said, and walked away.

"Nice meeting you," Mackenzie called. She waited until he'd disappeared behind the steel porthole doors. "Hot damn."

Sabrina slumped. "You see what I'm up against?"

"And you think that man doesn't want you?"

"He hasn't made a single overture."

Mackenzie stared after Kit. "He looks like the type to go in for a slow, teasing seduction," she said softly. "You're so lucky."

"Lucky? Does that mean you're letting me out of our deal?"

Mackenzie gave a start. Her thoughts seemed far away. "Oh." She looked across the table at her sister. "Umm, no."

"How can I possibly resist him?" Sabrina said with a soulful moan.

"I already told you. *Chocolate.*"

"That makes no sense. I ate an entire chocolate dessert two minutes ago and I can promise you that Kit looks just as attractive to me."

"You need to let the chocolate chemicals accumulate in your brain and bloodstream."

"Huh?"

"Look at it this way. How did the chocolate make you feel?" Mackenzie dabbed her lips with the napkin. "It was a fabulous dish, by the way. Kit obviously knows his stuff."

"That's for sure." Sabrina sat up with her hands in her lap, thinking of how she'd inhaled the pastry even though she'd never been a chocolate fiend. "I guess I feel sort of satisfied. Warm and happy. It's not quite an all-out sugar rush, but the chocolate gave me an emotional boost." *Or maybe that was Kit*, she thought. For a man who moved with a languid deliberation, being around him certainly zapped *her* with energy.

"Did you know there was a survey that said fifty percent of American women prefer chocolate to sex?"

"No way!" Sabrina gawked. "They're obviously not having the right kind of sex." She narrowed her eyes. "You're kidding me, Mackenzie. You made that up."

"It's true. I had to read lots of candy research for my old job."

Sabrina was catching Mackenzie's drift. "You are *not* suggesting that I feast on chocolate in place of sex."

"Uh-huh. Pretty much."

"Forget it." Sabrina waved her arms like an umpire. "I'm outta here." But she didn't leave.

"What's the alternative, Sabrina? Not only will you lose the bet and the ring, but you'll go back to falling into one brief relationship after another. It's your pattern." Mackenzie put on her I'm-saying-this-for-your-own-good expression. There were times it was hard to believe she was the younger sister. "You see a guy, you fall in lust, you think he's The One and a month later you're on the phone to me complaining that he's around all the time and you can't breathe. Sound familiar?"

"Yeah." Sabrina put her elbows on the table. "So?"

"The same thing will happen with Kit if you can't control your craving."

"I thought you said he'd go for the slow seduction."

"That doesn't mean he can resist if you go nuts one night and corner him in the kitchen to act out some crazy apron-stripping fantasy. He *is* a man, after all. It's up to you to say no."

Sabrina peered between her arms, head in hands. "I was never any good at that."

"That's why you turn to chocolate. Remember, I've seen the research. The chemicals that chocolate produces in your body are similar to the pleasurable effect you get from making love. Endorphins are released. Seratonin and caffeine and phenyethylamine—something like that. They're natural opiates." Mackenzie smiled. "To be fair, some scientists say you'd have to eat chocolate by the pound to truly be affected, but...whatever. I'm sure it would help a little."

Sabrina dropped her hands. She was skeptical. "So every time I get an urge to suck on Kit's tongue I should pop a Hershey's Kiss instead?"

"Right. What could it hurt?"

"My dental bill. And pretty soon I wouldn't be able to fit into Dominique's dresses."

"Pooh. You could stand to put on a few pounds."

Sabrina ate, but her metabolism was high and she burned the calories off, unlike Mackenzie, who was prone to curling up on the couch with a good book and a bag of butterscotch candies.

"Are you game?" Mackenzie prompted.

Sabrina shrugged. She had nothing to lose. "I suppose. But you're going in for that haircut as soon as I can wangle another appointment with Costas."

Mackenzie didn't hesitate. "I will, I promise."

"Do I really have to hold out for the entire year?" Assuming Kit was interested...

"That would be ideal. Of course, I could be generous and give you some leeway if he proposes before that—" Mackenzie stopped and laughed at her sister's horrified expression. "But I know that's asking too much. If the threat of losing grandmother's ring isn't enough of a deterrence, could you at least pledge not to jump in bed with Kit until there's a real, honest, emotional connection between you two? Get to know him as a friend first. You might be surprised how different making love with a friend will feel."

"Well, you always went on and on about what a good friend Jason was, but I don't remember you ever saying he gave you hot sweaty jungle love."

"Our love life was satisfactory."

Sabrina grimaced, staring at Mackenzie until she blushed. Anyone having merely satisfactory sex might as well gorge on chocolate instead, and they both knew it.

"Don't worry," Mackenzie said, deflecting the attention. "You and Kit have a different dynamic entirely."

"Whatever it is will probably burn out before we get to the bedroom when I put this chocolate plan of yours into action," Sabrina complained.

Mackenzie stood and slipped her handbag off the back of the chair. "Then it was never meant to be."

"Meant to be?" Sabrina didn't believe in soul mates and destiny. She believed in having fun while you could because who knew what tomorrow would bring. "Now you're sounding like Mom and Dad, with all their explanations for why their divorce didn't stick. But what do you want to bet they're arguing when they get off the cruise ship?" For their second honeymoon, Charlie and Nicole had booked passage on a lengthy transatlantic cruise. They were due back in another week.

"You'll see," Mackenzie said with blithe assurance. "By the time our parents' second first-year anniversary rolls around, all of us will know if we've been successful at changing our lives."

"A year is a long, long time."

Mackenzie squeezed Sabrina's shoulder. "Not when the rewards are worth the wait."

2

KIT WAS TRYING to convince himself that it wasn't necessary for him to find out firsthand if Sabrina Bliss lived up to her name. Some things were better left to the imagination. This was one of them.

This...*bliss*.

So why had he volunteered to help her move?

She hadn't asked for help. A couple of guys from the kitchen got the idea when she was recently telling them about finally finding an apartment after a month-long search. They'd roped Kit into the deal, and he'd been curious enough to agree. Sabrina came into the kitchen every day and watched him work, sitting silently on a stool, out of the way but very much on his mind. Usually he got into a zone when he cooked. The clamor of the busy restaurant kitchen faded away while he concentrated on molding chocolate tulip cups or icing a multilayered bombe. But Sabrina wasn't an unobtrusive type of woman. She shot his concentration to bits.

Kit and Parker and Vijay piled out of their cab in Chelsea, telling the driver to wait. Sabrina had been staying with her sister while she searched for an apartment. Mackenzie Bliss had a ground-floor flat in a gently aged brownstone with ivy crawling up the lintel. The street door was open. Kit checked the mailboxes in the vestibule and rang the bell for 1A.

The door opened as far as the security chain allowed. "Why, good morning," Mackenzie said through the two-inch gap between the door and jamb. Kit nodded. Parker gave her a broad smile. She shut the door, and the chain made a *chunk*ing sound when she slipped it free. The men crowded toward her as soon as she opened the door again. She stepped back, holding on to the lapels of her terry cloth robe. "Uh, hi, Kit. What's going on?"

"This is Parker..." A roly-poly sous chef with a deceptively cherubic face. "And Vijay..." A handsome young Indian who had a deft touch with sauces. "And we're here to help Sabrina move."

Mackenzie was clearly surprised, but she recovered to exchange handshakes with the other men. Kit admired her aplomb. Except for minor facial similarities, she was the opposite of her sister—shorter and rounder, softer and kinder, where Sabrina was sharp angles and bright eyes and frequently outspoken. Except around him. With him, she was quiet, observant, a little nervous. Her watchful eyes made him too aware of himself.

"Sabrina's not expecting you, is she?" Mackenzie let them in. They filed into a short, narrow hallway alongside two shoe boxes, a backpack, a suitcase and a rolled-up futon without a frame, not much thicker than a pallet. They were too early. The moving preparations had barely begun.

"It's a random act of kindness," Vijay explained. "Sabrina said to me she was moving this morning, so I came to be of assistance."

"Isn't that nice?" Mackenzie had a funny smile on

her face as she led them into the living room. "Sabrina? Your movers have arrived."

Sabrina entered, daubing a towel on her damp hair. She wore loose batik drawstring pants and a brief tank top that tented over her small, high breasts. Kit dropped his gaze to her bare feet, long and bony, then back up, drawn by the irresistible allure of perky, pointed nipples. Vijay was looking at the ceiling. Parker was looking in the same place Kit was, only his mouth was hanging open, showing a tongue wet with spittle.

A modest woman would have clutched the towel to her chest. Sabrina took a long look at the men, then bent at the waist to briskly rub her hair dry. She straightened, flinging the entire curly length of it back off her face. Her breasts moved beneath the top, rounding in the scoop neck before resettling, and Kit thought Parker was about to go into cardiac arrest. His own heart was jumping around in his chest like a caged monkey.

Unfazed, Sabrina threw the towel on the couch and put her hands on her hips. "Hi, gang. What's up?"

Kit looked at Parker who looked at Vijay who was still looking at the ceiling.

"They're here to help you move," Mackenzie said. She stepped farther into the small, cozy room and plopped into a cushy armchair with an unexplained chuckle. She crossed her bare legs, pulling the robe over them. Kit had the sense that she was accustomed to sitting back and observing her sister's untidy life with a fond, amused tolerance.

"Oh." Sabrina's nose crinkled. "All three of you, huh?"

"Muscle power," said Kit.

"Such beautiful ladies should not be lifting heavy boxes," Vijay said.

"The more hands we have, the faster it'll go." Parker forgot about ogling and cracked his knuckles. "Your new place is a third floor walk-up, hey? Big job."

"Not as much as you'd think," Mackenzie said from the depths of the chair.

"I appreciate the thought, guys." Sabrina came forward and gave Vijay's cheek a pat. "But it's not exactly necessary."

A lot of Kit's reactions to Sabrina weren't necessary, but he had them anyway. After undertaking years of travel and adventure while he tried to figure out his place in the world, he'd finally come to the point where he was ready to settle down and make a real home. By all rights, he should have been attracted to Mackenzie. She appeared to be precisely the kind of woman who would suit his new vision for his life. But he couldn't get Sabrina out of his head.

"We *want* to help," said a ruddy-cheeked Vijay.

"You might be fooled," Parker said, putting a hand on his midsection, "but this isn't fat—it's muscle."

"Of course it is." Sabrina reached out and squeezed Parker's biceps. "One-hundred-percent muscle."

"We're here," Kit said. "You might as well take advantage of us. We have a cab waiting outside, but we can also call for a van...."

Sabrina cocked her head to aim a smile his way, but she didn't turn toward him or touch him. He tried not to feel seriously deprived, especially when he saw the chili pepper tattoo on the back of her bare shoulder. That tattoo had been driving him crazy for a week, peeping out from under the straps of her sleeveless dresses and tops, never quite showing itself.

"The thing is," she said, "I travel light. Did you see the stuff in the hallway?" She gestured. "That's all there is, aside from a garment bag and bunch of cleaning supplies that Mackenzie's going to lug over so she can scrub out my new place."

"You don't have furniture?" Vijay asked, dismayed.

Parker was gleeful. "Man, this is the best moving job ever."

Kit clapped his hands, being brisk to cover up his dismay at discovering that Sabrina was as flighty and footloose as he'd suspected. "Let's load up then. Our cab's waiting."

He knew what it was like to travel light, had been that way himself for years. But he'd had enough of that lifestyle. Everything had changed for him a couple of months ago when he'd stood over a gravesite in Cleveland and said goodbye to the only family he'd had left. Now that he was completely and utterly alone, he finally understood how important it was to make a bond, to build a family, to have someone to hold on tight to.

First step was finding that someone.

Sabrina Bliss was the slippery type. Not what he was looking for.

"I can do it myself," she was insisting, but the men were already discussing who should take which end of the futon. Kit solved the problem by slinging the awkward bundle over his shoulder. "Wait, let me get my shoes," Sabrina said as he grabbed a string-tied shoe box and headed out. Mackenzie had already run off to the bedroom to change.

The luggage and the shoe boxes went into the cab's trunk. Kit had to wedge the futon, folded like an over-stuffed crepe, into the back seat. Sabrina loped out of the brownstone in sandals, her damp hair flying behind her. She climbed into the cab with her garment bag and a big straw satchel, sliding herself into a space beneath the futon.

Kit asked the driver if it was okay for a passenger to sit up front. "Mackenzie?" he said, opening the door.

She rattled down the stoop with a mop and a broom and a bucket filled with assorted cleansers, dressed in comfy sweats with her house key held between her teeth. "Mmph."

He got her settled, then peered in the back of the cab. "Room for one more—the muscle of this operation."

Vijay and Parker bumped into each other trying to get there first, but Kit moved nimbly past them and bent one end of the futon so he could squash it down and fit inside, his legs arranged like puzzle pieces. "Take the next cab," he said, winking to the losers as the taxi drove away.

Sabrina stared straight ahead for a silent minute. "But Vijay doesn't have the street address," she said after they'd turned the corner onto Ninth Avenue.

"Damn," Kit said cheerfully. Her thigh was pressed against his and he could feel the dampness of her hair seeping into his T-shirt. Her shampoo smelled like flowers in the rain.

Sabrina didn't seem too concerned. "I guess we can manage on our own." Her eyes slid sideways toward Kit. "Seeing as the muscle's here."

Mackenzie hooked a hand over the seat back as she turned to speak to them. "But that was rude, leaving

Parker and Vijay at the curb when they were nice enough to..." Her voice trailed off when she saw that Kit and Sabrina weren't really listening.

They were looking into each other's eyes, pushing the rolled and folded futon down across their laps. "I'll make it up to them," Sabrina murmured.

"I'll buy them beers after work." Kit had never been this close to her. Her lashes were brown, and one of her eyes was slightly darker than the other, hazel mottled by green and gold flecks. Her nose was narrow, with a sharp tip, but her mouth looked soft, especially when she wet her lips. She didn't have on a speck of makeup and he could see a couple of freckles and tiny dots of moles, plus a thin white scar on her chin and small lines around her mouth—imperfections that made her even more perfect. He thought that she was the kind of girl who wouldn't care if her hair got tangled in the wind. She would exchange fun days in the hot sun for a few extra wrinkles later on. She'd laugh and frown and wear her expressions on her face without scheduling Botox injections first.

The lonely boy inside Kit wanted her as a friend. The man on the outside simply wanted her.

"You can come, too," he said, "for beer."

"I have the whole day off." Her mouth, which was wide, became even wider when it stretched into a quick grin. "I needed it to make my big move, although I may have exaggerated the undertaking to Dominique and Curt."

"You do have to wait for the cable guy. That could take all day."

"Not on a Sunday. Besides, I don't have a TV. Maybe

I can wangle another day off to wait for the phone guy."

They could have a fling, Kit thought. Sabrina was a flingy kind of woman. Just because he hoped to settle down didn't mean every date had to be taken with serious intentions. It would be okay, spending several weeks, maybe a month—or two—with Sabrina. From the little he knew of her work history, and going by the severe lack of possessions, she didn't stick with anything for long. She'd be ready to move on before he started feeling too serious about her. They'd go their separate ways, no harm, no foul.

A perfectly imperfect solution.

"So you're saying you have a free day with almost nothing to do?" Kit eyed Sabrina.

She'd turned her face away, but he could see her very flirtatious, very female smile. "I wonder what I should do with myself. Any suggestions?"

"You're forgetting the cleaning," Mackenzie said, raising her voice above the traffic.

"That should take an hour." Sabrina glanced at Kit. "Not only is my new place a scuzzy rat hole, it's an extremely small scuzzy rat hole."

"Welcome to the Manhattan working class." He touched his fingertips to her leg, feeling the heat of her skin through the thin cotton pants. The scratchy seat of the cab thrummed beneath him. "What should we do with the rest of the day?"

"*We?*"

"I'm not working until the dinner shift."

"Umm." Sabrina jiggled her leg and he lifted his fingers away for an instant before dropping his palm over her thigh, soothing the pent-up energy that ran through her like an electric current. He heard as her breath caught short, then released in a luxurious sigh. "Umm. I suppose *we'll* have to think of a way to entertain ourselves."

At her low velvety purr, Kit's libido leaped right past thoughts of homey comforts and women who'd make good wives and mothers. Parker had been right—this was the best moving job ever.

"Stop!" Mackenzie suddenly commanded from the front seat. "Stop. Right here, in front of the candy store."

The car screeched across a lane of traffic and pulled halfway into an illegal parking spot by a fire hydrant. "Mizzy, I can't stay here—" the driver beseeched as his passenger jumped from the cab.

Kit gaped at what had caught Mackenzie's attention. The display window of the narrow storefront was piled high with gold boxes and trays of chocolates in all sizes and shapes. Sabrina leaned past the futon, took one look and muttered a dire warning under her breath.

Mackenzie slammed the car door as she got out. "I'll only be a minute. I need to buy my sister a housewarming gift." Suddenly her face loomed in the open back window, serious with a disapproval Kit didn't understand. "A nice big box of *fudge*."

"No, THIS ISN'T the closet," Sabrina said, triumphantly throwing open the door of her third-floor flat after a delay that had entailed a journey into a dark, dank basement to hunt down the super and receive her new keys. "It's the apartment."

The wall opposite was so close it bore scrape marks

from the front door. Kit edged in backward, dragging the futon. He expected to see a room opening off the narrow hall, so it took him a few seconds to understand that the hall *was* the room. It widened by several feet on the right—that was the living room—and culminated in a tiny stove and a sink built into the wall on the left, which was the kitchen. The scarred doors midway in between might open onto a vast ballroom with skylights and a light-filled conservatory, but he was betting on a closet and airplane-sized bathroom. Although the ceiling over the living area was high, it slanted sharply, giving the space an odd lopsided feel.

There was only one place to put the futon. He dropped it beneath a double-hung window covered with filth so thick it served as soundproofing as well as an effective sunblock. A layer of black soot lined the sill. It was only May, but already the apartment was airless and stifling.

Mackenzie hauled in the cleaning supplies. She carried the enormous box of fudge to the kitchen, took one look at the stained sink and said, "Sabrina, are you sure about this? I'll loan you the money for first and last if you want to get a bigger place...."

"Nonsense. If I'm going to be responsible and live within my means, this was the best I could find in a safe neighborhood. You can think of the place as an atelier, if that helps. I'll give the walls a coat of paint and it will be fine for a year." She glanced at Kit. "Or at least a few months."

Stepping on the futon, Sabrina flicked the latch and tugged on the window. It didn't budge. Kit shoved hard on the upper sill and it opened with a screech of the ancient wood and a shower of paint chips. The view was of electric lines looped to the backside of an old button factory on West End Avenue. An enormous water tower loomed beyond the neighboring brick ledge, which threw a shadow into the apartment.

Sabrina wilted. "I'll paint it sunshine yellow."

"If you want to live in an egg yolk. Personally, I'd paint everything a bright, clean white. And put up a lot of mirrors." Mackenzie approached the taps with caution. The pipes clanked when she turned on the water, then spurted out a stream of rusty water.

Kit lugged in the suitcase and the backpack. Sabrina hung her garment bag in the closet and put her shoe boxes on the open shelves above a built-in dresser. "There you go. I'm all moved in." She dusted off her hands. "Yet another benefit of traveling light."

"How do you live without accumulating stuff?" Mackenzie asked over the sound of rushing water filling her bucket. "Don't you read? Listen to music? Cook?" She dumped in half a bottle of Mr. Clean. The stagnant air grew sharp with ammonia.

"I give books away when I'm finished with them. I go to clubs for music. Pots and pans I leave behind for the next tenant."

Kit leaned across Mackenzie to open the kitchen cupboards. "You're going to need new ones now. These are empty." Except for the roaches, scuttling toward the cracks and crevices.

Sabrina had regained her optimism. "Good—a reason to go to the flea market."

Kit thought of the displays of stainless steel cookware in Williams-Sonoma. Glasses, china, silver... He could outfit her kitchen faster than a bridezilla with a scanner in one hand and a registry in the other. But Sabrina would probably hate that.

Could he have a fling with a woman who didn't know the joys of copper-bottomed sauté pans?

One look at her bending over to unzip the suitcase answered that question. *Hell, yes.*

In the other direction, Mackenzie was down on hands and knees scrubbing out the undercounter refrigerator. Her rear end was better than Sabrina's, from an objective viewpoint. He gazed thoughtfully, but aside from a pleasant moment of appreciation for the female form, Mackenzie's backside did little for him.

"What are you looking at, Kit?" Sabrina stood watching him, a small tarnished bronze horse statue in her hands.

"I was wondering where to put a dining table."

"I don't need one. I'll eat cross-legged on the futon."

"Too many crumbs. You'll get roaches."

"She already has roaches," Mackenzie said under her breath.

"That's not civilized," Kit insisted. He'd hated the stuffy sit-down dinners at his guardian's house, but then a few years later when his last-chance foster mother—a Frenchwoman known to all as Ma'am—had laid down the law that her kids must be home for dinner every evening, he'd come to look forward to the tradition. Even though on arrival he'd rudely sworn he'd break every rule she set. A proper dinner and the conversation and connection it established between the "family" had ended up being a rule that held deep significance for him.

"You definitely need a table," he said.

"I might be able to wedge a bistro table in here. Or I could put it on the fire escape."

"And when it rains?"

"I'll eat at Decadence."

"We can fit one in the hall, here, if the table's narrow enough. Very, very narrow—a console." He measured the space with hand spans. "The chairs would have to tuck under or there'd be no room to walk by."

Sabrina shrugged. "Good thing I'm skinny."

The comment drew his eyes to her like a moth hurtling into a flame. He could almost hear the snap and sizzle of his single-minded desire hitting the blaze. Her golden hair had dried into rippling waves that skimmed over her shoulder blades. The red pepper tattoo flashed at him, then disappeared when she twisted and turned. He loved watching her move— bending, lifting, stretching to place items from her shoe boxes on her freshly scrubbed shelves, every motion suffused with the athletic grace of a ballerina.

"What now?" she said, catching his eye.

"Were you ever a dancer?"

Her eyes danced while the rest of her went still. "Are you telling me I look anorexic?"

"No. But you could use some fattening up."

Mackenzie sat back on her heels. "Sabrina's the ecto-morph of the family." She swiped the heel of a rubber-gloved hand over her brow. "I've learned to accept that."

"Ah, but you're sisters—both attractive, in your own way." Kit reached for the broom. "It's just my cooking gene showing. You have an instinct to nest, Sabrina has one to roam, and I want to stock and furnish this sad excuse for a kitchen."

Having emptied the suitcase, Sabrina zipped it shut and trundled it into the closet. "I can't get used to being around all these men who cook," she said from inside the door. "If only the average husband knew how attractive their wives would find them if they put on an apron now and again." She poked her head out and winked at Kit. "Tell me, do you have groupies, huh?"

He batted her gorgeous backside with the broom. "Only you."

"That's what you think," she said with an airy laugh. "Actually, I'm only interested in the chocolate."

He raised a wicked eyebrow. "Hmm. Is that so?"

She blushed. Must have remembered previously admitting to her sweet tooth deficiency. "It is. Now that I'm in restaurant management, I have to develop my taste buds."

"I'll cook for you anytime." He hadn't meant for his voice to lower, but it had, making the offer more suggestive than friendly. Sabrina swayed toward him, her eyes liquid and alive.

Mackenzie gave a discreet cough.

Sabrina was quick to back off, blinking. "That won't be necessary, thanks. The super told me there's a Korean grocery around the corner. I'll go later and pick up a few staples."

"There's always the fudge," Mackenzie said. "A piece a day keeps the testosterone away."

"What does that mean?" Kit asked, sensing an undercurrent between the sisters. They were up to something.

"Oh, nothing you'd want to know about, Chocomeister." Sabrina's voice was too innocent. "Wowza," she said, "there's a giant spider web in here. With mummified remains and all. Give me that broom." She held out an open hand, her long fingers motioning to him from around the closet door.

Kit came up behind her. "Aren't you afraid of spiders?"

"Not at all. I've lived in too many hovels to squeal over every creepy-crawly creature that appears." She lay her hand on his forearm. The hair on it prickled even after she'd released him, muttering a throaty "Sorry."

He slid in beside her, making as if he was examining the web, but actually consumed with the sweep of her hair over his arm, the warmth of her body so close to his. The sound of her breathing filled the closet. Was it short? Was it shallow? Was she as aware of him as he was of her?

"Do you have a paper?" he croaked.

"Umm." Sabrina left the closet, but was back in an instant, handing him a white square. "A paper towel."

He took it, angling toward the spider web. She leaned with him, her arm resting across his shoulders. "What are you doing?" she whispered. "Just kill it. Stomp it."

He touched the paper towel to the web, coaxing the fat spider onto it. "Out of my way."

Sabrina nimbly stepped aside. He carried the paper towel to the open window, turning it over as the spider crawled along the edge toward his fingers. He shook the towel outside, over the fire escape. "Go, little spider. You've been set free."

"Free to build a new web on my fire escape," Sabrina said, elbows propped up on the sill beside him. A touch of a breeze fingered through her hair, blowing

strands of it across his face. She drew it back behind
her ears in the way that women did, making a ponytail.
The neck of her top gaped a little, displaying her collar-
bone and the shadowed hollow between her breasts.
He imagined touching her there, with his fingertips.
Tasting her, with his lips.

Her mouth curved. "So...the mystery man reveals a
soft heart."

"I'm no mystery man."

Her eyes engaged his. "And your heart?"

"Give it a little time," he said. "Maybe you'll find
out."

AN HOUR LATER, the three of them sat in a row on the
thin futon, looking at the apartment, freshly cleaned
but still sadly bleak. Mackenzie and Kit had stretched
out their legs. Sabrina's knees were drawn up to use as
a desk. She was making a list on the back of a dry
cleaner's receipt.

"Pillows," Mackenzie said.

"Pots and pans," said Kit.

Sabrina scribbled. "One pot, one pan. I'm doing a
minimalist thing."

He let out a windy sigh. "Utensils."

"A comforter," Mackenzie added.

"Mixing bowls."

"Towels. Tissue. Bath oil."

"Wait, wait," Sabrina said, amused that all of her sister's items were for comfort and all of Kit's were for the
kitchen.

"You'll never carry that much alone," he said. "I'm
coming with you."

Mackenzie passed the fudge. Already Sabrina was

sick of the stuff—her sister had constantly urged it on her—but she took a piece anyway and nibbled it as she completed the list. "There's no way I'm buying all of this at once."

"Most important is food." Kit waved the fudge away with a grimace. Out of politeness, Mackenzie had offered it to him every time she'd forced it on Sabrina. "Food *other* than chocolate."

"Left to her own devices, Sabrina will come home with two oranges, a loaf of bread, a jar of peanut butter and a bottle of water." Mackenzie tapped one sneaker against the other. "Maybe I should come along to help you shop."

"Oh, please! I'm not a baby. Thanks for the offers, guys, but I can manage on my own."

Mackenzie leaned closer to whisper behind her hand. "*On your own* isn't the issue."

Sabrina turned her head away from Kit, lowering her voice. "I'm stoked to the gills with chocolate. Don't worry."

"You're a big girl." Mackenzie got to her feet. Kit joined her. "Umm, I just remembered I can't go with you anyway," she announced, giving in graciously. "I have a meeting this afternoon with my builder. We're finishing up renovations on my shop. Going over the final budget today, so I've got to be there." She stuck out a hand. "Nice to see you again, Kit. Thanks for helping Sabrina out."

They shook hands. "Should I go down and whistle for a cab?" he asked.

"That'd be great. I'll be right there as soon as I gather up my stuff."

"I'll take the bucket and mop."

Sabrina watched Kit go, big and broad and manly in a lank T-shirt and jeans. Perspiration-damp black hair curled over his ears and forehead. He looked happy and cheerful, almost like the boy next door, although as an adult she'd never had a next door for longer than a few months at a time. The serious, reserved persona he wore in the restaurant had peeled up at the edges like his hair, giving her a good long look at the man beneath—warm and caring in an earthy, sexy way.

"I don't like the way you're looking at him." Mackenzie stood in the doorway with her broom. She'd left the detergents and scouring pads lined up on the two square feet of available counter space. "If you owned a spoon, you'd be eating him up."

Sabrina swiped her brow. "Oh, please. Not a chance after all that fudge."

Mackenzie shrugged off the assurance as she glanced toward the stairs. "I don't blame you about Kit. He's quite the man. I think he'd be really good for you—"

"Good," Sabrina scoffed.

"But try to resist, okay? If you fall back into old habits now, next thing I know you'll be packing for Zimbabwe or some other far corner of the globe, and I've been really looking forward to having you around for a while."

"Thanks." Sabrina gripped her sister in a big hug. "Me too."

Mackenzie smoothed Sabrina's hair from her face. "After today you've *got* to stay away from Kit."

"Then why did you set me up with him for your store opening?"

"I don't know. I wasn't thinking. Maybe it was to

test your mettle. Or sabotage. I do love that ring, you know."

"That's cruel."

"It's not that I don't want you to see him. You can even date. Just don't sleep with him."

"But he's so yummy."

"So is chocolate. Go in and have another piece."

Sabrina made a choking sound. The first few squares of rich, sweet fudge had gone down easily and possibly even increased her sense of well-being. But her interest in Kit hadn't lessened. The only benefit was that by the fifth piece, she'd begun to feel sick. Physical attraction had momentarily been trumped by faint nausea. She suspected the former was longer lasting.

"Mackenzie," she ventured, "I have to say that this idea of yours is not working."

"Then we need to find better chocolate. I know of a small candy company that sells Better Than Sex chocolate bars. I'll have a month's supply delivered ASAP."

"Uh, thanks."

Mackenzie kissed Sabrina's cheek. "It won't be forever." She gave her another squeeze. "Abstinence is good for the soul. And chocolate satisfies every desire."

"Who said that?" Sabrina asked as Mackenzie departed. "Gandhi? Mother Theresa? St. Valentine?" She hung over the stair rail. "I'm no saint!"

Mackenzie's voice floated up to her. "It must have been Willie Wonka."

Sabrina groaned. "Well, damn. Dip me in a vat of Godiva and call me a virgin, why don'tcha?"

3

"SEE HOW PLUMP IT IS? Feel this. So firm." Kit took a deep sniff before thrusting the tomato at Sabrina. "Smell. You'll think you're smack dab in the middle of a garden."

Sabrina inhaled. Mmm. Kit was right—she was home in Scarsdale in the tangled, weedy vegetable patch her father had planted among her mother's manicured perennial beds. The sun was hot; she wore braids and Lolita sunglasses; there was an itchy scab on her knee from a skateboard accident and loud voices drifting from the house....

Chomp. She took a giant bite out of the ripe tomato. Juice squirted over her cheeks and chin.

Kit's surprise gave way to an exuberant laugh. He lifted the tomato to his own mouth and bit into it. A glop of seeds and juice ran down his wrist. "Delicious," he said, raising his arm to slurp it up. "We'll take a dozen." The lady who ran the produce stand shoveled tomatoes into a clear plastic bag.

The bite of warm red flesh slid down Sabrina's throat. "I can't eat a dozen tomatoes at once."

Kit was stalking the eggplants. "Sure we can."

We, she thought, scowling to hide her unreasoned joy. She followed him closely, watching as he hefted eggplants and thunked melons.

"Two of the aubergines and one honeydew." He

dropped the melon he'd chosen into a bag extended by the proprietor. "For your breakfast," he told Sabrina, offering her the half-eaten tomato.

Not *our* breakfast. She took a small bite, avoiding his fingers.

"Here, you're sticky." He pitched the rest of the tomato into an overflowing trash can and asked a passerby for a spritz from her water bottle so charmingly the girl laughed and obliged, squirting his hands. He dabbled his wet fingertips over Sabrina's chin. "There. That's better."

"Now I'm dripping." Ducking, she pulled her tank upward, drying her damp face on the front of it like a child.

Kit's gaze had dropped to her exposed midriff. "I can see your—" He swallowed. "Ribs."

She tugged the shirt back down. "Is this what it's like, hanging with a chef? They follow you around saying, 'Eat, eat. More, more.'"

"That's an Italian mother."

"Or a Jewish one."

"Or Greek."

She smiled. "Chefs must all have mother complexes. Only, being men, you feed the world and get well paid for it."

Kit passed money to the vegetable lady and received the heavy bags of produce. At other stalls, he'd bought onions, mushrooms, too many peaches and apricots and a huge bunch of glossy red grapes.

Loaded down with parcels, they made their way through the throng of weekend shoppers at the farmer's market. The door stood open at a small bakery, emitting smells of rising yeast and hot bread. Kit ducked inside and came out with a baguette of French bread wrapped in a narrow paper bag, holding it above his head like a triumphant warrior.

Sabrina shook her head at his glee and said, "Enough already. Come on, we'll have to get a taxi instead of the train," but he was already distracted by another vendor with baskets of fresh herbs that spiced the air with traces of mint and basil and oregano.

"I'm getting a cab," she yelled over her shoulder. Her arms were so weighted she felt as if they'd stretched six inches. She pushed through the festive crowd, bags bumping. Kit came running, meeting her where the stream of shoppers dispersed among the bustle of traffic on Mulberry. Setting the bags of fruit and veggies on the sidewalk, she lifted a hand to signal for a cab.

"Five minutes," Kit said before disappearing again.

She looked behind her at a drab storefront with a striped awning. Beyond a dingy window in which thick lengths of sausage hung, Kit consulted with a fat man in an apron. The butcher's tattooed arms waved as the discussion grew involved. Finally he clapped Kit on the shoulder and reached behind the counter.

A cab screeched up to the curb and she loaded her parcels into it, climbing in herself as Kit emerged with a paper-wrapped bundle. "I got the last real Italian chorizo," he said, panting as he pushed in beside her. "It's the best in the city."

"I'll take your word for it." She was a goner if Kit should ever decide to seduce *her* with the passion he showed for their groceries. Hard to believe she'd considered him reserved. He was a different man away from the restaurant—less intense, not so contained.

The teasing hints of playfulness she'd detected at Decadence were now full-blown, and very appealing. While they shopped, he'd dropped amusing little stories into their conversation, telling her of truffle-hunting expeditions with a pig and a man named Hogg in the south of France, of learning to make risotto and pears in mascarpone custard from a nun in Siena. Sabrina could have listened forever. She was intoxicated by the heady delight of really *liking* the person she was hot for.

But now here she was, all worked up without a bite of chocolate in sight. That was the one food item they had not purchased.

"Umm..." She nudged Kit's shoulder. "What do you expect me to do with all of this food?"

"I'll show you."

"So you're not only a pastry chef?"

"Of course not. That's my specialty, but I can cook anything."

"Even without dishes and utensils?" she said, remembering. She'd had no chance to drag out her shopping list—Kit had pulled her from one stall to the next as soon as they hit Little Italy. She'd been sure there were farmer's markets closer to her neighborhood, but he'd insisted the trip downtown was worth the hassle.

"I went into a store when I sent you to buy the eggs." He rummaged through the purchases until he found a shopping bag with string handles. "This will get you started."

The bag crinkled as she peered inside. A flat pan, three whisks—why three?—a bundle of cutlery, stainless steel mixing bowls. "Thanks, but I'll reimburse you. For all of it," she added, mentally wincing at the balance in her checking account. New York was expensive. A large deposit on the apartment had eaten most of her savings. Mackenzie frequently offered loans, but Sabrina wouldn't take them. It was a matter of honor— she'd survived this long on her own, even if she didn't have a portfolio or hefty retirement account to show for it. Security wasn't important to her. *La dolce vita* was. Turning thirty didn't *have* to change that.

"Consider it a housewarming gift," Kit said.

On impulse, she brushed her warm cheek over his, whispering thanks. "I'm overwhelmed."

"Wait until you taste lunch."

He was coming back to her apartment, then. He would fill it up with his wide shoulders and his deep voice and his sheer presence. She shouldn't have been so happy at the thought. Normally she hated being crowded. Some of her finest days had been spent on the beach at Baja California, where she'd stayed for two months in a hut without real walls, only bamboo blinds that she rolled up to let in the sunlight and the salty sea breeze.

The city was teeming and uptown traffic was slow, but eventually they arrived at her new apartment. For a moment, she was dismayed at the idea of a year of dwelling in the heavy brick building, cloistered off the alley in what was essentially a closet with a toilet and a window. Then she remembered the pulse of the city, the vitality that had surged through her. It would be okay. She was on another adventure.

Kit unloaded the bags, extended his hand. *Her sojourner*, she thought, placing her palm in his.

"Where do you live?" she asked as they entered her

building and climbed the stairs, weighted down like pack mules.

"A midtown sublet. It's nothing special. I got the place from another chef who moved for a job in L.A., but it's only good for five or six months. I've been there four. I'll look soon for a permanent home."

"You plan to stay in the city?"

Kit stopped outside her door. "Don't you?"

She looked at him over the rounded end of the crusty loaf. "Not—" Her bargain with Mackenzie was supposedly going to last a year. The first five weeks had been spent on finding the right job and the wrong apartment. She'd been lucky when an old friend in the food service industry had recommended her to Dominique Para, who'd been willing to count Reno cocktail waitress and roller-blading hot-dog queen as job qualifications. But that didn't mean Sabrina was so grateful she'd commit to the long term. Even a year was iffy. Extremely iffy, if Kit hung around and she lost the bet. No reason to stay after that. Unless Kit became the reason.

"Not forever, no," she said quickly—and defiantly. "I like to stay footloose and fancy-free."

He nodded. "Right." Their camaraderie had suddenly dimmed, and it wasn't because the super was too cheap to replace the burned-out lightbulbs in the ancient fixtures.

Disappointed, but not quite sure why, she juggled her packages to free a hand and slid her key from the pocket of her drawstring pants. She inserted it into the lock. "Aren't you the same?" Clutching fruit to her chest, she pushed open the door.

Kit's eyes had gone the color of a rain-chopped river. "What gave you that idea?"

"Dominique happened to mention it. She said you've worked all over the place in the past." Dominique hadn't been the only one. Parker had quoted Kit's résumé to her one day when they'd shared a cigarette in the alley behind the restaurant. They'd both been awed by the world-class restaurants that had hired Kit.

"Join the Navy, see the world," he said, standing aside while she shoveled Mackenzie's detergents in the space under the sink. They started unloading. Soon fruits and vegetables covered every inch of counter space.

Sabrina turned on the water, eyeing the muscled terrain of Kit's chest and arms while they waited for it to run clear. "You were in the Navy? I don't see any anchor tattoos."

"Should I take my shirt off?"

Her heart thumped. "No, thanks. I don't need proof."

"I see you have one."

She hitched her shoulder. The tiny chili pepper tattoo on the back of it was a souvenir of a night in Tiajuana with a man whose kiss she remembered but whose name she'd forgotten.

"It's cute," Kit said, looking at her.

Stupid, cramped apartment. They were standing too close. She could feel the heat of his body. See the hint of blue behind his thick lashes, the glint of the gold at his ear. Even though they hadn't kissed, his name was already tattooed on her brain. *Damn—where was the fudge?*

"You look hungry," he said. "Have a grape."

She grabbed the entire bunch and thrust it under the water.

He picked up the strays. "You should have a colander."

"I don't know what a colander is."

"Liar."

She held up the glistening grapes, waggling them to shed droplets. "Drip-drying works."

"What about your hands? We didn't buy towels."

The comment made her think of wet naked bodies, but he appeared oblivious, splashing at the sink. She worked on sweeping him out of her mind while he washed the tomatoes, put them in one of the new mixing bowls and dried his hands on his jeans.

And she still hadn't stopped dwelling about wet naked bodies. A distraction was in order. "When were you in the Navy? Dominique didn't mention that at all."

"After high school—sort of." He looked uncomfortable. "So Dominique gave you a rundown on me, huh?" They both knew that Dominique was willing to gossip indiscriminately, although she was more discreet about staff since they led less interesting lives than her gadabout friends.

Sabrina blushed. "Okay, I confess. I asked her."

"Why?"

She backed up to the counter. Licked her dry lips. "I think you know why."

Although his feet didn't move, suddenly he seemed right there on top of her. She was focused on his eyes, but she felt the rest of him through her pores. Hot, male, predatory, his chest—no, his entire body—

slowly expanding and contracting with each deliberate breath.

"Because you like me," he said in a low voice that melted her like butter. He lifted a hand. It hovered over her bare arm, making the hair on it rise. She almost expected him to start crackling like the wand of a metal detector. Certainly *she'd* been set off.

Parting her lips and making a response seemed to take forever. Her voice came out as soft and scratchy as an old record album. "Yes...I like you."

"You want to date me."

"Mmm." If that's what he called it.

"Maybe you want to kiss me."

Maybe? For sure!

His eyes were so hot on hers it was like having her head dunked in his double boiler. She made a rough sound in her throat that probably passed for assent; it was all she could muster.

Kit lowered his fingertips onto her arm. His touch was silken as it glided upward. "And I want to kiss you," he whispered, holding her face in both hands now, tilting it as his mouth came down over hers. The kiss landed softly. He lipped her, gently plucking and lapping, his palms cradling her cheeks. It wasn't what she'd expected, but it was...*heavenly.*

Her fingers closed on his wrists, holding her up when her knees started to give out. She was in full swoon—all thoughts, all feeling centered on Kit's kisses, which were so sweet and deliberate she believed he was savoring her.

His arms went firmly around her, one hand bunched in her hair, holding her fast against his chest as the kisses deepened by minute degrees. His tongue was liquid and warm. She gripped him tighter, lost in the molten flow.

"Ma chérie."

She swam partway out of her lovely stupor. "What? Do you speak French?"

"A little." He tried to keep kissing her, but she pulled back. "I'm a chef, after all. I went to cooking school in France."

Yes, she'd known that. Even Dominique was impressed. Two years at the Cordon Bleu and then apprenticeship with someone whose name she couldn't pronounce.

"So you're a sailor who speaks French..."

"Only while French kissing," he said with a soft, tumbling chuckle. He licked at her bottom lip.

"What else do I need to know about you?"

"That I'm wild for you." He swept her into a tumbling stream of kisses, each more delicious than the previous. Eventually she had to force herself to turn aside, pressing her forehead to his shoulder. He gave a soulful moan and buried his face against her neck, drawing in a breath as if he were inhaling her.

Sabrina shivered. Her frustration was acute as she clung to him. Going against instinct to fight the desire, her mouth opened and she bit down—not hard, but not soft—on the swell of muscle in his arm. She needed—oh, she needed him...

"No." She pushed away. Hands outspread, she scrambled through the parcels on the countertop, then flung open the small refrigerator. The fudge! She grabbed the gold box and crammed a piece into her mouth. It was hard, cold and too sweet. Couldn't hold a candle to a kiss from Kit Rex. Mackenzie was crazy if

she thought chocolate was a cure for this gnawing sexual hunger.

Brows raised, Kit watched Sabrina consume the fudge. "If you like it *that* much, I can make you a fudge brownie that will blow your mind. I melt the darkest, purest chocolate anyone's ever seen, so precious they sell it by the ounce, fold it into a mixture of—"

"Nmph!" Sabrina said, waving.

"I'll give you the recipe."

She swallowed a lump of the stuff. Her tongue remained coated in chocolate. She rolled it against her lips, smacking. Kit tasted better. *No. Stop. Distract yourself.* "Thanks, but I don't cook."

His eyes were half-lidded, his gaze fastened on her mouth. Even after all the fudge she'd consumed, there was a hollow in her stomach. Nerves, she thought. She'd always been the high-strung type.

Except that she hadn't felt empty when she was kissing Kit. Nor light. She'd been anchored by him—*to* him—and had loved it.

"I can't date you," she blurted, even though technically she could. It was just that she knew where dating him would lead....

"Why?"

"Mackenzie." Sabrina smoothed the torn waxed tissue paper and gold foil over the remaining pieces of fudge, replaced the lid and put the box back in the fridge. She swallowed, tasting chocolate residue. Her so-called sex substitute had worked that much, anyway—replacing the intoxicating flavor of Kit's nimble tongue. But she doubted that it was fudge she'd be thinking of tonight in bed.

"Mackenzie?" he echoed.

"I made a promise to her."

"About me?" Kit worked his hands through his hair, leaving the dark curls in an attractive jumble. He kept his arms upraised, elbows akimbo, fingers knitted at the back of his neck. He wore an understandably stunned expression. "I don't get it."

"Not you, in particular. The promise pertains to all men." Sabrina picked up the melon, avoiding his eyes—and swollen fly. God, men were blatant creatures. "Mackenzie and I made a sort of pact to change our lives, and my side of it was to lease an apartment, find a good job, hold on to it for at least a half a year, and—" She stopped, swallowing again. More chocolate, less Kit, that was what she needed.

He waited.

She rolled her eyes toward the ceiling. "And give up men."

A long moment passed before he responded.

"Dammit," he said, swearing softly as he slid his hands into his pockets, shoulders hunched, "and I'm a man."

He was *the* man. She sneaked a glance at him. His T-shirt was rucked up and the waistband of his jeans had slid lower with the thrust of his fists, revealing an inch of hard flat tummy. His skin was smooth and lightly tanned. She wanted to touch it so much her hands shook.

Smiling, he cocked his head at her. She gritted her teeth. The man was impossibly confident. And damn if he wasn't looking at her as if she was the funniest joke he'd heard in a long time.

"Couldn't you have given up fudge instead?" he said. "You seem to have all the symptoms of a fudge addiction. Shaky hands, sweating brow, nervous eye twitch." More teasing.

She would *not* tell him about the role chocolate played in her pact with Mackenzie. He'd probably break a rib, laughing so hard.

She sniffed. "You're the chocolate expert."

He took a half step toward her. His hand slid across her abdomen, fingertips grazing the line between shirt and skin. "Ahh. So this—" his palm slipped lower, across her belly button "—is the way to your heart?"

"Wrong direction."

When he whispered in her ear, the velvety richness of his voice made her head spin. "You'd rather I touched your heart?"

"That's not what I—"

"Is this the spot?" He breathed against her cheek as a delicate fingertip stroked the hollow of her throat. His other hand dropped to her rear end. "Here?"

"No..." She couldn't put together a coherent thought. "Not that, either." *Oh, man!* "Please stop touching me. Everywhere."

He instantly removed his hands and she was able to breathe again. Breathing had lost the top spot on her list of favorite things to do, but what the hell. If she couldn't have Kit...

"All I'm allowed to offer you is chocolate?" he asked, mystified.

She gave a stiff nod. "Right."

"That bites. And not half as well as you do."

Not going there. "We can be friends."

"Friends? Bah. You only want me for my way with chocolate. All that talk of your lack of sweet tooth was obviously a cover-up for your secret motive." Kit began washing more of the fruit in a workmanlike way, getting rid of the clutter to clear counter space. He nudged her over, setting out one of the new mixing bowls and flipping open the carton of eggs.

Sabrina sagged against the edge of the sink, wishing she had a kitchen chair. Even a stool. A tuffet. It wouldn't look good if she gave in like a spineless jellyfish and sank to the floor. In a space this tight, even a little naughty horseplay came across as a stampede. No wonder she felt flattened.

"Were you a cook in the Navy?" she asked when the silence grew too long. Chumminess was the way to go. They could pretend they hadn't wanted to suck each other's lips off.

"Didn't start out to be, but that's where I ended up." He cracked six eggs into the bowl. More eggs than she normally ate in a month.

"What did you start out to be?"

"Anything *but* a cook. I was eighteen—it wasn't macho to wear an apron, so I was willing to try anything else. I wasn't the college type, so I enlisted. The Navy was supposed to help me overcome my strange attraction to powdered sugar and ganache."

She laughed. "Obviously, it didn't work." He had no idea how appealing a man in an apron could be. "You're saying that you were into cooking as a teenager, before the Navy? How did that happen?"

"It started as a punishment. Ma'am assigned me to kitchen duty."

"Did you say *ma'am*?"

"That's what all the foster kids called her. Françoise Herbert O'Neill was her name. She was a French Canadian, emphasis on the French, who'd married a

Buffalo vacuum salesman. She had five children of her own and then started taking in foster kids as soon as her oldest had gone off to college. Said she did it because she wasn't about to settle down into boring middle age if that meant crocheting and bingo. She wasn't your typical American housewife."

"She sounds wonderful to me."

He nodded. "She was."

"Was?" she questioned. His voice had cracked, almost inaudibly.

"She passed away about two months ago."

Kit had kept his profile to Sabrina, but she could still see how deep his sorrow went. It was in his voice, his lowered eyes, in the way his fingers momentarily fumbled with the whisk. "I'm so sorry," she said.

He stopped whisking the eggs, but he didn't look at her. "I went back to Cleveland for the funeral."

Something in his tone made her veer off in another direction. "What about your real parents?"

"Out of the picture." Kit clipped the words off. "They died a long time ago."

"I see."

He started whisking again, seeming to shake off the melancholy. "My becoming a chef was all my foster mother's fault. I gave Ma'am hell when I arrived at her house. I was nearly sixteen by then and I'd been in and out of a few foster situations and even a stint in Juvy. Thought I was a badass. My plan was to take off as soon as I had a driver's license and could legally quit school. In the meantime I wasn't about to stick to the strict house rules set up by a whacked-out French dame." He smiled to himself, beating the eggs into a yellow froth.

"Rebelling against the rules," Sabrina mused. "Sounds familiar."

"I bet you were a handful." Kit glanced at her, his smile becoming wicked again. "Still are."

She blinked, astonished at the way her nipples tingled in anticipation of having his hands on her breasts. "Get back to Ma'am and the rest of your story."

"Yes'm." He rolled a red bell pepper across the counter at her. "You want to help out and chop that up? There should be a knife with the cutlery. Nothing like my set of French knives, but it will do."

She rinsed off the knife, then dried it with the edge of her tank top while Kit grumbled about forgetting to buy hand towels. "You said you were sentenced to KP?"

"I'd broken a rule as soon as I arrived—probably a slew of them. Ma'am was cooking for a household of seven at the time, so she always needed kitchen help. I started out peeling potatoes." He lifted the drooling whisk. "Of course, KP wasn't just KP. Those hours in the kitchen gave Ma'am an excuse to get closer to the foster kids that were in the most trouble."

The pepper stung Sabrina's nostrils. She wrinkled her nose. "Did you fall for that? Chatting about your confused feelings while snapping peas on the back porch?"

"Oh, I resisted. I was surly. Sometimes I skipped out entirely." Kit gave a short laugh. "But I also kept breaking Ma'am's rules. Eventually…"

"You got to like kitchen duty."

"Yeah. It was the first extended contact I'd had with a normal home life in a long time. You know, the TV blaring, kids roughhousing in the other room, pots bubbling on the stove. A mother figure bustling around the kitchen, stirring soup and asking nosy questions."

"I had that—some of the time." Sabrina poked her tongue against her cheek as she sliced tomatoes onto a plate. Life in the Bliss household hadn't been *only* about marital discord. There'd been many good times when she and Mackenzie were younger, times filled with family outings, jokes told over the dinner table, cozy board games by the fireplace. "You never did?"

"Not so I remembered. Not until Ma'am."

"She was a good cook?"

"I told you, she was French. To hear her tell it, the terms are interchangeable."

Kit turned on the electric stove. The first burner he tried was out, but the second one worked. "Somehow, over the next few months, she got me interested in food. When I stole a bottle from her husband's wine cellar, her punishment was to sit me down for lectures about oak casks and grape fermentation. We even did a wine testing."

He paused and his expression was affection-ate...tender. "Ma'am said I had a good nose and a discerning palate even though it was woefully uneducated." He shrugged. "I was needy enough to be flattered."

A lump rose in Sabrina's throat.

"Are you finished with that? Chop up some of the chorizo next, and then you can do the onion."

"Oh. Yes." She sniffed.

"Hold it under the water and you won't cry."

She didn't cry. She'd given up sentiment when she was thirteen years old.

Kit went on. "So I broke another rule—I think it was staying out past curfew—and learned about bread-making. Then I broke another rule, and another—" He chuckled. "You get the idea. I wasn't about to admit outright that I wanted to learn to cook. But Ma'am knew. Especially when it got to the point where I barely bothered to hide my crimes."

Sabrina remembered how she'd flaunted her own bad behavior, thinking she was tough, but underneath hoping that her actions would prove to her mom and dad how much she hurt. Instead she'd only caused more discord.

She cleared her throat. "It's hard to fool a mom. They have that third eye."

Kit's brows went up. "Hmm?"

"You know. At the back of their head. Every time I tried to put one over on my mom, she knew." Except when Nicole Bliss had been so wrapped up in the on-going divorce that she hadn't realized her oldest daughter was floundering just as badly. Sabrina had lost her horse when they had moved out of the family house and could no longer afford riding lessons, yet that had been only part of her upset. The easiest to express.

But Kit. Look at him. He'd had it worse....

"I knew there was an explanation for you," she mused.

"What does that mean?" The ingredients were all chopped and a dollop of butter had melted in the pan. He lightly sautéed the chunks of sausage and vegetables, then poured in the egg mixture, let it firm up and added tomato and sprigs of fresh parsley. Cooking smells filled the apartment. Her stomach rumbled, even after all that fudge.

"It means that you're a combination of bad boy and mama's boy," she said with a lilt. "Now I know why."

He tore the tag off a spatula, shooting her a look that sizzled her at the edges, like the omelette. "That's me." He flipped half of the puffed omelette over onto itself. "Devil in an apron."

Great. And *she* was sworn to be a nun.

4

Despite Kit's obsession with a dining table, they had ended up sitting on the futon, eating the omelette straight out of the pan. After his third reminder to be careful not to scratch the new pan with her fork, Sabrina had accused him of fussing like an old woman. At the back of her mind had been the idea of starting something up with him. She'd even ripped off a chunk of bread, scattering crumbs everywhere, but he'd only laughed and started talking about paint colors for the walls.

My own brilliant fault, Sabrina thought the next day at work as she stood at the captain's podium surveying the busy restaurant. The place was running like the proverbial well-oiled machine, wouldn't you know? Not a single crisis from the waiters or kitchen staff. She had no excuse to go back and see Kit.

Served her right. She'd fought him off too successfully. It was nice to know that he was the type of guy who listened when he was told "Hands off," but then again...

Surreptitiously, Sabrina scooped a couple of fingers into the cup of M&M's she'd stashed on the shelf behind the telephone. She faked a cough, raising her hand to her mouth to slip the candy-coated pieces inside. Cheap, short-lived relief, but not as heavy as the fudge. After hearing about Kit and Sabrina's first kiss over the phone, Mackenzie had brought over a jumbo-sized bag of the candies. Sabrina had salted the M&M's away in every conceivable access point—her pocket, her purse, behind the bar—but they weren't helping.

Kit was constantly on her mind.

Her lips still burned from his kisses.

The rest of her…

She reached again for the candy. Aside from the promise to Mackenzie, the diamond ring was also at stake, even though Sabrina wasn't sure why she wanted it if she had no plans for marriage. Sentimental value? A good luck token? Her late grandma's marriage had lasted for over sixty years, so that had to cancel out the next generation's divorce. But what would she do with it even if she managed to win it? She couldn't hang a family heirloom from her keychain. The ring was better suited to Mackenzie, not her.

A handsome older couple approached the podium, requesting a table. "Mrth?" Sabrina said around the chocolate in her mouth.

"Two," said the fellow, smiling broadly, his teeth whiter than his hair.

Sabrina ducked her head and chewed fast while she slipped two menus from the stack. "Umm, how fortunate." Swallow. "We do have an open table, party of two."

The man put his hand on the woman's elbow. He was dressed in a navy blazer and Princeton tie; she wore a pale gray dress as conservative as Sabrina's. "Party of two, that's us, isn't it, my darling?"

Sabrina smiled as she seated the couple. Their obvious long-term togetherness cheered her, when normally she'd be worrying about when the husband would try to pat her butt. Who knew why? It wasn't as if she'd changed her mind about the sanctity of marriage. "A server will be along shortly. Please enjoy your lunch."

The wife put out a hand to Sabrina. "Miss? This is rather awkward, but I must tell you." She lowered her voice. "There's something on your—" She tapped her front teeth.

Sabrina clapped a hand over her mouth. "Excuse me," she muttered before hurrying across the restaurant to the ladies' room. She leaned over the steel vessel basin and bared her teeth at the mirror. Horror! They were rimmed with chocolate.

This was *not* the image Dominique expected her to project.

Sabrina sucked the chocolate from her teeth, then wet her fingers under the arched faucet and rubbed them clean. A few droplets had spattered the front of her dress, so she crossed to the hand dryer and angled beneath it, aiming her breasts at the burst of hot air.

A patron entered, a young girl whose scruffy hair and jeans contrasted with designer accessories. Her bored expression didn't change when she saw Sabrina's contortions. "Go for it." She waved, disappearing into a stall. "Whatever gets you off, lady."

Sabrina straightened. "Lady?" she mouthed at her image in the mirror. Her cream-colored dress was another of Dominique's. It was sleeveless, but the straps were just wide enough to cover her tattoo. Her hair was braided and wound into a tight little knot at her nape. The only jewelry she wore were small gold studs in her ears.

It was true. Normally she was a girl, a chick, a hot

babe, sometimes even a hoochie mama. Now she was a *lady*.

Ugh. Maybe losing the bet with Mackenzie wouldn't be such a bad thing. Then she could have Kit *and* freedom.

Or would that be Kit *or* freedom?

Sabrina put the temptation out of her mind and hurried back to work. Ninety minutes later, business had begun to slow and she could have spared a few minutes to slip into the kitchen. Kit would be starting preparations for the evening's desserts and she did so adore watching him melt chocolate....

"Sabrina, love." Dominique Para swept into the restaurant, carrying a shopping bag from Barneys and wafting perfume and minty breath spray. She kissed the air near Sabrina's cheeks, *smack, smack*. "How's business?"

"We had a good—"

"Hellooo, wonderful man!" Dominique called, waving at a balding middle-aged Wall Street icon who looked eager to exchange stock tips on a personal basis. He bobbed halfway out of his seat.

"What *is* his name?" Dominique said through her teeth, holding her smile. Sabrina opened the reservations book to check, but as usual Dominique didn't wait for an answer. "Who knew millionaires would be so boring? I'm going up to the office so I don't have to make small talk." She stroked a wrinkle out of the front of Sabrina's dress, sniffing suspiciously. "Has our Kristoffer been feeding you chocolate again? Never mind. Come up to the office when you're free—I have fabulous news!"

Sabrina cupped a hand over her mouth and puffed

air into it. Yep. Chocolate breath. Maybe she could bor-
row some of Dominique's mouth spray.

"Send me up a martini," Dominique said to the bartender as she flew by, aiming toward the private stairs
at the back of the restaurant.

Sabrina took care of a few tasks, then dragged Charmaine away from the Wall Street guy's table to say she
was going up to the office for a chat with the boss.

Regretting the missed opportunity to melt in sync
with Kit's chocolate, Sabrina stopped by the bar to
fetch Dominique's drink—she popped in a few olives,
all the lunch that the slender ex-model would probably
get—and headed for the stairs.

"I'm parched." Dominique waved Sabrina into the
small office. She had her feet propped up on the desk,
the better to admire her recent purchase.

"Nice shoes." Sabrina placed the martini in Dominique's extended hand.

"Aren't they?" Dominique lifted a leg, flexing her
calf and pointing the arrow-tip toe of the hot pink
pumps. The heels were ideal for a shoe fetishist, sharp
and steep. In the wrong hands—or feet—they could be
a lethal weapon. "Curt made me swear not to use the
business card for personal purchases, but what's the
use of being a restaurateur if I can't run up the expense
account?"

"Then you'd better hide the box." The shoe box lay
open beside Dominique's discarded shoes—also hot
pink pumps, but with a slightly less dangerous heel.

Dominique sipped her drink. "Not necessary. Curt
will forgive me when he sees this heel."

Sabrina nodded. The other owner of Decadence was
also a former model, and as mad a fashionista as Dom-

inique. Curt Tyrone was six-five, devastatingly hand-some, bald and black—or, as he preferred to say, *mocha.*

"Take my old shoes, if you'd like. I've only worn them twice." Dominique liked to share her good fortune. She'd loaded Sabrina up with a gorgeous wardrobe in the same way, with a casual grace that had saved Sabrina from feeling awkward about accepting hand-me-downs.

"Have a seat." Dominique stretched languidly, crossing one famously long leg over the other. She gazed over the rim of her martini glass, her clever lips pursed. "Guess what? I've landed us an international fancy-schmancy society gig—and I'm putting *you* in charge."

Sabrina dropped into the low Barcelona chair. "What?"

"You're shocked." Dominique swung her legs off the desk. "Did you think I'm here strictly for ornamental purposes?" She laughed huskily. "I do have my uses. Take my international connections. All these years, I may have appeared to be flitting around the globe with no purpose but looking good on a runway. Such was not the case. And one of my favorite charities has come through for us big-time—"

Dominique paused dramatically with a toss of her silky black bob. "Do you know the International Relief Organization?"

"The IRO. Sure."

"I was their spokeswoman in the early nineties. I posed for ads, but I also visited refugee camps and spoke before Congress."

"Yes, of course," Sabrina said. She vaguely remembered the famous shots of the glamorous model Dominique Para posing with a group of grimy, poverty-stricken children, looking less than glamorous and all the more beautiful for it.

"To make a short story long, imagine what a shock it was to run into my old roommate Daffy DeMarche at a spa last month. She used to be Daphne B, catalog underwear model, before she married into a society family, but we don't mention that. It turns out that she's the chairperson of this year's IRO awards luncheon. It took three lunches and an afternoon of shoe shopping, but I've persuaded her to give Decadence the catering contract." Dominique swung back and forth in her neon-green padded leather swivel chair. "Isn't that great? I know you'll do a super job."

Sabrina gulped. "Me?"

"Didn't you say that you put in a whole bunch of years with the IRO volunteer corps, teaching English or plastering mud huts in some godforsaken village?"

"It was only six months. A college program. I was in South Africa, distributing food and medical supplies."

Dominique fluttered bony fingers. "You see? You're perfect for the job. Don't be modest," she said, blocking Sabrina's protest. "As a fabulous creature and proud of it, I deplore baseless modesty."

Sabrina had to laugh. She knew that her boss's flamboyance was mostly facade. Dominique was from Hobb's Corner, Kansas, and had been discovered by a modeling scout as a six-foot fourteen-year-old, buying Lipsmackers in the local mall. Her present age was as indeterminate as the faint lines on her nearly flawless face, though it had been whispered that she was approaching forty-five. She'd never married. The general belief was that the partnership with Curt Tyrone was friendship-based, but no one knew for sure. It was one of the rare subjects on which Dominique and Curt were mum.

"As a less than fabulous creature, forgive me for having doubts." Sabrina bit her lip. "I'm not sure I can handle such a big event. I'm not particularly experienced...."

"It's all about confidence," Dominique said. "You have that. It's not every woman who could arrive for an appointment with me wearing an ill-fitting Ann Taylor suit and still get the job."

Sabrina squirmed. The suit had been a loaner from Mackenzie. Dominique had spent a good portion of their interview describing the Decadence "look." She'd be horrified if she knew about Sabrina's real wardrobe.

"But, Dominique. I have no idea where to start."

"With Daffy, of course." Dominique slipped a card out of a tiny red silk pocketbook shaped like a pair of lips. "Here's her number. You call, she'll give you the number of her second-in-command and off you go!"

Sabrina reached for the embossed calling card.

Dominique must have caught the subtle eye roll. "I know, I know. Keep in mind that one must never expect the chairperson—or one's boss, for that matter—to do any of the actual work." With a shudder for emphasis, she flicked her hair off her shoulders and stood. "Well, I'm off." She stepped over the open shoe box and the discarded shoes without a glance. "I have an appointment for a bikini wax with a rather large, terse Russian woman and I am *not* looking forward to it."

Dominique swept out the door and down the steps. Sabrina contemplated the discarded pink shoes, then her own. She'd gone too many years in bare feet, flat sandals and sneakers to be comfortable in high heels. Then again, every woman in Manhattan seemed so fashion-conscious—even Mackenzie, now that she was seeing a stylist, aside from her reluctance to get rid of her schoolgirl hairstyle. And the shoes would do great things to her legs. Kit might notice.

The pumps were practically new. The soles were barely scuffed. Sabrina toed off her own serviceable taupe flats and tried Dominique's shoes on. They were impractical and flirty and frivolous, with little grosgrain ribbons at the heel.

She stood, wavered slightly, then found her balance. What was it about high heels that made women preen and men drool?

She stuck out a leg, posing like Dominique.

Fabulous. Kit would *definitely* notice.

KIT PEERED OUT of the porthole of the swinging doors, looking for Sabrina. When he saw her walking gingerly toward the bar, he ducked out of sight, then two seconds later was back in place, watching as she eased onto one of the chrome-and-maple bar stools that had been conceived more as art pieces than comfortable seats. She spread her receipts across the bar, chatted briefly to the bartender, then crossed her legs, hooked a heel on one of the spokes of the stool and got down to work.

Kit stared at the flashy pink high heels, certain she hadn't been wearing them earlier. Had she changed just to torture him?

He tugged at the collar of his white coat. The dry

cleaner had used too much starch, but the damn collar wasn't the only thing that felt too stiff.

"Keep standing by that door and you're going to wind up with a broken nose," Parker called from across the kitchen.

Then he'd have gotten off lucky.

Kit took the warning and moved away, forcing himself to go back to work. His assistant had the crème brûlée well in hand and the test batch of mousse cakes were already in the oven. Kit began to prepare the custard topping, but his mind refused to stick to ingredients as mundane as vanilla and eggs.

Sabrina had bewitched him with her mercurial ways. He'd lost hold of his convictions.

Frowning, he turned up the heat beneath the custard. Before Sabrina, he'd been sure that his goal to settle down was the right thing to do. Ma'am's sudden death several months after he'd returned to the country from Tahiti had knocked him for a loop. He'd visited her first thing, of course, and had noticed that she'd slowed down a lot in the years since her husband had passed on. Although her grown children had also offered, Kit had been ready to turn down the job offer at Decadence to live in Cleveland to take care of her. But Ma'am had been as stubborn and independent as ever. She wouldn't hear of him giving up this chance and had insisted he go on to New York. He'd agreed, seeing how proud she was of his success.

He'd hoped she'd be able to travel to Manhattan to see the restaurant, but a bout with a virus had forbade that. And then the cold had turned into pneumonia and she'd died.

It had been a strange thing, how unanchored he'd

felt by the loss. Other than the distant memories of his folks, for as long as he could remember he'd believed himself to be alone, even after Ma'am had helped him to change the direction of his life. Until the funeral, he hadn't fully understood how much he'd counted on her presence, like a safe harbor mapped into his heart even when he wandered thousands of miles away. Without Ma'am, he'd truly been at sea.

So he'd conceived of a solution: to find a good woman, marry her, buy a house, have several children. Be happy. Be content. Be weighted down again.

Then came Sabrina, light and sassy, sashaying her trim little behind.

She was so wrong for him, and yet he couldn't stop wanting her. Even if he managed to persuade her to quit eating chocolate long enough to hop into bed, he had a sneaking suspicion that a fling might not be enough for him. And that it wouldn't be the best course of action for her, either. Despite the flippant exterior, he'd detected hints that she was more fragile than she let on.

"Excuse me." Vijay tapped Kit on the shoulder. "Is that custard scorching?"

Kit started, dropping the spoon he'd been holding in the air. He grabbed a dish towel to protect his hand and shoved the pan off the heat. "Damn." He'd forgotten to stir.

With the kitchen staff ribbing him, he scraped the ruined custard into the garbage. His assistant made an exaggerated show of checking the timer on the mousse cakes and removing the tray of ramekins from the oven. The individual mousse cakes had risen perfectly, but remained soft in the middle. He tested one with his finger.

Charmaine came in from the dining room and plopped into Sabrina's place, observing Kit's unusual distraction. She touched the corner of her mouth with the tip of her tongue, then sucked it back in. "She's getting to you."

"Nope," he said. "She's got me."

"Wow. Usually men can't recognize that."

Kit shrugged. "What do I do now? She doesn't want me."

Charmaine only laughed.

"Maybe she wants me," Kit conceded. "But she doesn't want to keep me."

"Not to worry." Charmaine fluffed her pink hair. "Sabrina's no dummy. She'll figure out that you're a keeper." The waitress smiled as she gave him a blatant onceover. "Mmm-mmm. Good thing you're not my type."

THE SMELL of baking chocolate kept distracting Sabrina from adding up the lunch receipts. She leaned her head against her hand and huddled over the calculator, punching in numbers and trying not to drool. Mackenzie's chocolate scheme had turned her into Pavlov's dog, slavering at the scent of sweets. Add in the thought of Kit, sugaring, melting, mixing, flexing…

I will resist.

"Are you almost finished?"

It never failed—Kit's voice always made her quicken inside. "Yes," she said, pressing a button for her total. $1,621,344.89? Decadence had been open for little more than a year and was still considered a hot spot. The afternoon totals were usually impressive, but they weren't doing *that* well.

Hurriedly, she shoved the receipts into an untidy pile and looked up. "Hello, Kit. How may I help you?"

He stood behind the bar in the familiar white coat and passed a small dessert plate along the polished stainless steel surface. "Be my taste-tester?"

She looked at his offering. "What is it?" *More chocolate. Just what she needed.*

"A mini chocolate mousse cake, served with a Marsala-laced custard, garnished with bittersweet chocolate curls and a dusting of cocoa powder."

Oh, my. He might as well mainline pure powdered cacao bean directly into my veins.

"It's not appealing?" Kit asked when she didn't respond.

Her forced smile became genuine when she looked into his eyes. His brows were doing an I'm-so-cute-when-I'm-unsure squinchy thing and she couldn't resist.

"Oh, no. Very appealing," she said, picking up the fork he'd provided. She'd eaten fruit for breakfast and had skipped lunch, except for the multiple handfuls of M&M's it had taken to keep her out of the kitchen.

She dug in. "Yum," she said through a mouthful of the dense chocolate concoction. It was delicious—sinfully rich and still warm as it melted on her tongue. The custard was the perfect contrast. Within seconds, she felt the happy chocolate glow seeping through her bloodstream. Her cheeks flushed with pleasure.

Kit leaned closer, putting his elbows on the bar, his hands loosely clasped. His eyes were trained on her face like twin laser beams. "It's good?"

She moaned. "It's utterly orgasmic. Women are going to be climaxing all over the restaurant when they taste this dessert. You've outdone yourself."

"Climaxing, hmm?"

She put down the fork and pinched her eyelids. When would she learn to watch her words? "Did I say that?"

"I think you've just named this dessert." He gave a low, sexy chuckle. "Sabrina Bliss, meet the Chocolate Orgasm."

She sputtered. *Oh, if only!*

The miniature cake was so delicious she ate every crumb, regardless of her surfeit of chocolate. Fortunately, the serving size was small. Even the most stringent of dieters would be lured to have a Chocolate Orgasm once word had spread. "This is so good it could be our signature dessert," she said, trying to think business instead of sex.

"No, we already have the Decadence Brownie. I might save this recipe for my own place." He winked. "Don't tell Dominique and Curt that I'm experimenting on their dime."

"You have ambitions to open your own restaurant?" No surprise. All the chefs did. They spoke of financial backers with the same reverence they held for Julia Child and fresh mahimahi flown in from Hawaii.

"Not a restaurant. An old-fashioned French chocolatier."

"Ah."

"I've been saving for it. You see, I'm not merely a ship passing you in the night. I have prospects."

"You're selling them to the wrong woman," she said. "Because I *am* a passing ship." Didn't hurt to remind him of that. Even if the disappointment in his eyes made her stomach revolt against the chocolate chemicals.

She couldn't change her beliefs. Not without proof.

Her longing for the family engagement ring didn't count.

"Pardon me," Kit said, whisking the plate away. He'd put on the stony face he got when he didn't want to show his tender side. "I forgot."

Remorse drained the endorphins of her chocolate high. "That doesn't mean you can't tell me about it," she rushed to add. "What are your plans? I'd really like to hear them."

"Some other time."

"No, now. Really. Do you have a backer?"

"I don't need a backer, I hope. Opening a small shop is less involved and costly than a restaurant. I'm a diligent saver, and I have a broker friend who handles my portfolio. Even the recent downturns in the stock market haven't been too hurtful."

"Oh." For every aspect of her and Kit's personalities that meshed, there was another that was opposite. She searched for an intelligent comment, but Wall Street wasn't her thing. "We had a big whoop-de-do financial guy at lunch today, at the prime table. An admirer of Dominique's. Ivar Whitman."

"Him? He just got out of prison."

"Then I guess I shouldn't take the investment advice he offered."

"What was it?" Kit asked, looking wary.

"Plastics," she said, quoting a late-night movie she'd watched at Mackenzie's, *The Graduate*.

Kit laughed. "Eh, he was only trying to impress you."

"Little does he know, I'm more impressed by a Chocolate Orgasm." Her gaze lowered to Kit's chest. Most of the chefs looked like Pillsbury Doughboys in their double-breasted white jackets. Not Kit.

"Then maybe we ought to get together and—"

"Don't say it." Sabrina squeezed her eyes shut for an instant. *Chocolate, don't fail me now.* "We're just friends, right? Isn't that what we agreed on?"

"I don't remember signing an actual agreement."

"Well, I have. So there will be none of this 'getting together.'"

He started to protest, but she waved him off, desperately searching for a different tack—one that would point out their differences, not their chemistry. "Ahem. Funny you should mention savings. I remembered just the other day how I'd once saved a lot of money. Well, a lot for a kid. It was probably the only time in my life I planned for the future."

She went on brightly despite Kit's obvious disappointment at the brush-off. "You see, I was one of those horse-crazy little girls. I hung out at a local riding stable every day. Finally my parents let me start real riding lessons. That did it. After the first one, my goal in life was to own a pony or a horse. Mom and Dad said it was too much money, but they also wanted to teach me responsibility. Finally they agreed to pay for the horse if I could save enough for the other expenses, like tack and stable fees. They probably didn't expect me to stick it out, but I was dedicated. I saved every penny—allowance, lunch money, baby-sitting jobs.

When I turned thirteen, the stable hired me to muck out stalls.''

She stopped and took a breath. What had started as a distraction was becoming revealing. Old, suppressed memories were rising up, and she was surprised by how much power they still held.

"Don't quit there," Kit said, leaning his arms on the bar again. She had the feeling he'd have reached across to take her hand if she'd given even the smallest sign that she was willing.

She was, but couldn't let it show. She glanced around the restaurant. Still peaceful in the lull before the early diners would arrive. Past time for her to clear out, but suddenly she *wanted* to tell Kit about how much Tory had meant to her.

"I had my eye on a nice little horse. Victory Banner, but his stable name was Tory. He was thirteen, like me. The prettiest sorrel, the color of a caramel apple, with a flaxen tail and mane. I adored him. I persuaded the owners to sell, withdrew my savings, drew up a budget of the expenses and was planning to present the plan to my parents as a done deal when—''

She choked up. Kit made a soothing sound, but she shook her head, battling back the sharpening memories. "I was so excited when I came running home from the stable that day. But I knew as soon as I got in the house that something was wrong." She blinked, but her tears were drying up. "Mom and Dad called Mackenzie and me into the living room. They sat us down and announced they were getting divorced. We'd have to sell the house. Looking back, I can see how selfish it was, but all I could think about was that I wasn't going to get my horse after all and that my parents had ruined my life. Major trauma." She shrugged. "Kids."

Kit didn't say anything for a long while. She winced, imagining that he was comparing the troubles of a pampered little suburban brat with his own stint as an orphaned foster child.

"It was probably easier for you to focus on the horse than the breakup of your parents."

She sighed. "I guess."

"What happened then?"

"Nothing, really. Mom and Dad split. We sold the house and moved into a cheaper one. Mackenzie and I spent weekends at our dad's apartment nearby. The stable was too far away—I never went there again."

"And your savings?"

She dredged up a smile. "That was why I started this story, wasn't it? Well, let me see. In the next year, I ran wild, acting like your typical teenager, thirteen-going-on-twenty-one, or so I thought. The money was frittered away on new clothes, nail polish and ankle bracelets. I was determined to be as irresponsible as possible." She checked his expression. "What a complete brat I was."

"It's understandable. Why do you think I got into fights, committed vandalism and stole cars?"

Her brows raised. "Whew. You were a real juvenile delinquent. The worst I did was shoplift."

"Yeah, we were a couple of really bad kids. And look at us now."

She laughed uncomfortably. Damn. This wasn't supposed to happen. Her little tale of woe had swung around on her and led her back to a bond with Kit. He was looking at her with a kindness that went straight to her heart. But then he didn't know that if Mackenzie hadn't instigated the bet, Sabrina would still be living out of a suitcase and acting as irresponsible as ever.

"Water under the bridge." She shrugged. "My shift's up. I'm going home."

"Tired?" Kit asked as he straightened.

"Not really. This isn't exactly the most strenuous job I've ever held. Not on a par with mucking stalls."

"Good. Because before you interrupted me I was going to ask if—"

She minded being insulted by his amorous attentions?

"—we should get together to paint your apartment," he finished. "It's so small, we can be done in an hour."

Sabrina thought of how she'd sobbed in her pillow the night of her parents' divorce announcement. She thought of them cruising off into the sunset, the second time around. She thought of Mackenzie and the bet and the symbolism of the diamond ring she couldn't bring herself to let go of.

She thought of chocolate.

Then she thought of sex.

It should have been the other way around. Because when she opened her mouth, her chocolate-induced willpower had ebbed so low she couldn't stop herself from saying, "Sure. Why not?"

Oh, double damn. She *knew* why not!

5

KIT WAS ON THE MARK about the painting. In an hour, they'd painted every surface in sight the compromise color—a buttercream that was halfway between white and yellow. Privately Sabrina thought it looked like French Vanilla ice cream, but anything was better than chocolate. Leaving her limited possessions stuffed in the closet, they painted themselves right out of the room. After washing out the rollers in the basement, they hit the street in paint-daubed clothing. No one dressed up for the flea market.

After a fast ride, they emerged from the subway into the light and walked to a flea market on Canal Street, their strides matched. It was a fine New York City day and Sabrina was feeling good. As long as they kept busy, she wasn't thinking about her strong attraction to Kit. Of course, every time she stopped what she was doing and looked at him—as she did now, over the shelf of a stall selling lots of chipped enamelware—she got a funny feeling in the pit of her stomach.

She thrust a hand into the pocket of her baggy track pants, just to check. One emergency Better Than Sex chocolate bar, slightly melted.

Kit must have felt her gaze on him, because he let loose with one of his I've-got-a-sexy-secret smiles and started toward her. Suspecting his purpose, she hurriedly picked out a rounded pitcher and held it up between them. "What do you think?"

He stopped and put a finger on the lip of the jug, where the white enamel had flaked off to show the black underneath. "It's chipped."

"So what?"

"Wouldn't you prefer new?"

"Not really. And my pocketbook sure doesn't."

He scanned the stall with a dubious expression. "Okay, not new. But at least we can choose pieces that aren't cracked or chipped."

"Have you looked at the prices? I can only afford the imperfect ones." She wrapped her arms around the pitcher, hugging it to herself like a mother with an ugly child.

"If you say so."

She chose a couple of coffee mugs for a quarter apiece. The rust rings were on the bottom, not the inside. "Think of them as well-loved."

"Worn out, you mean."

"Don't be a snob. You are not getting me near the shiny kitchen displays at any of the big department stores."

"I can't help it—I'm a chef. I want you to have quality tools." Playfully he shielded his eyes from the blackened pan she'd spotted. The tag read $1.

"I'll take it," she told the seller, adding a few more of the cheapest items, including a scratched ladle and a slotted spoon that she'd probably never use but liked the idea of. She could put them in the pitcher with the whisks Kit had bought. A strangely domestic notion. Hanging out in a restaurant was a bad influence on her.

She handed over a ten dollar bill. "There you go," she said, giving Kit the shopping bag of clanking bits and pieces. "My kitchen is complete. Let's go look for sheets and blankets."

"You're not buying those from a flea market."

"Why not? I'm sure they've been washed. If not, I can wash them. With bleach, to get rid of the cooties."

Kit gave her a look. And she immediately thought of being naked with him, wrapped in sheets. Maybe he was right—secondhand sheets wouldn't do. "Okay. Forget the sheets. But am I allowed a blanket? Maybe a nice, soft quilt, stitched by someone's Grandma Flora Mae?"

He slung his arm around her shoulders. "Sure, but Grandma Flora Mae quilts come expensive these days."

They strolled around the flea market, enjoying the festive air and the variety of goods being sold—everything from yellowed ten-cent Valentines to thousand-dollar armoires. Eventually Kit was drawn to a booth that featured the Country French style. Yellow embroidered tablecloths, white lace curtains, glazed clay pottery, kitschy ceramic roosters. He lingered over a display of antique chocolate molds, then dug into a mound of textiles and assorted bedding and pulled out a quilted coverlet. "Perfect," he said.

Sabrina was surprised. The coverlet had loose threads and a watermarked corner. But it was also a lovely faded ecru color and intricately stitched. She smoothed her hands across the soft, worn cotton. "I like it."

"Reminds me of home," Kit said with a shrug, seeing her curiosity.

"Your parents?"

"No, Ma'am's house. She had blankets like this on all the beds."

"Mmm." She wondered why he didn't mention memories of his parents. "When were you put in a foster home?"

"Fourteen." He turned away to examine a wire egg basket.

Old enough to have memories. She spoke to the vendor and quickly paid more for the coverlet than she'd have spent for a new comforter in one of the discount chain stores. "Why?"

Kit was broody, his brows pulled low. "You should have bargained for a better price."

"Didn't want to." She folded the coverlet over her arm. "Are you going to answer my question? What happened when you were fourteen?"

"My aunt and uncle decided they didn't want me anymore. But who could blame them? I was an ungrateful houseguest. Are you hungry?"

She accepted the change of subject. "Starved."

"I smell hot dogs."

"Don't tell me you eat hot dogs."

"That was the first thing I did when I got to New York. Don't tell Dominique. She thought I was being discriminating about the food at Nobu. Truth was, I'd eaten three hot dogs at a sidewalk cart before we met, so I could only pick at the meal she bought."

They approached the hot dog cart and Kit ordered two, fully loaded, along with orangeades.

Sabrina ran her fingers over the scalloped edge of the quilt. "Tell me, at this fancy dinner, did Dominique make a play for you?"

"Why do you ask?"

"Two attractive people—it stands to reason."

"Would you be jealous if she did?"

"I might."

"Aren't she and Curt a couple?"

"They are? I thought he was gay."

"Oh." Kit scrunched his eyes. "Really?"

"Then *he* didn't put a move on you either?"

They laughed. "You didn't answer my question," Sabrina said, taking the foil-wrapped hot dogs while Kit paid the vendor. "Is that a habit of yours I should know about?" They walked along the street, looking for a place to sit, leaving the flea market behind. They settled on the graffiti-ridden cement stoop of an aged apartment building, where they'd be dappled by the shade of a chestnut tree.

Kit gave her a napkin and a drink with a straw poking out of it. "I prefer to keep my own counsel, as they say."

"Hiding secrets?"

"Just being private. I know that's not fashionable in a society of confessional reality shows and tell-all autobiographies."

"You told me about Ma'am." Sabrina peeled back the foil on her hot dog. "And then I told you about Tory. You see how it works? We keep exchanging stories and eventually we—" She stopped, suddenly aware that she wanted to say, "Fall in love."

Instead she bit the hot dog, chewed, and said, "We get to know each other," through the stinging taste of horseradish.

It was an astonishing thing, this idea of her sister's:

Getting to know Kit before she slept with him. There might even be something to it.

"Odd theory, coming from a woman who travels with a futon strapped to her back."

"That's not fair." She snickered. "You make it sound as if I should be setting up trade on a street corner."

"I didn't mean it that way."

"Eat your hot dog." She sucked the too-sweet orangeade through the straw.

He munched. "How much do I have to know about you before I can kiss you again?"

She hesitated, biting at the end of the straw. In spite of the friends-only ploy, her having sex with Kit was inevitable now that she knew he was interested. It was only the ring that made her delay. The best she could do was to hold out as long as possible. When Mackenzie finally went through with the haircut—which would be soon because Sabrina had finally secured another appointment—she'd be gracious in triumph. Of course she would. Mackenzie was always gracious. But she'd also be disappointed and ever so slightly judgmental. It'd be the same refrain: *Oh, that Sabrina! Sabrina can't help herself. Sabrina has no control.*

"Knowing me won't change a thing," she fibbed. "Friends are platonic. We're going to be platonic."

Kit frowned. "That's rot. Makes sense, there being an *ick* in *platonic*." He leaned over, bumping his shoulder against hers. "Are you sure? I'm a good kisser."

"I'm sure." Her stomach was jumping, and it wasn't because of the horseradish. "Friends do not kiss," she insisted, being uncharacteristically stalwart.

"Then I'm pretty sure I don't want to be your friend."

She fingered the chocolate in her pocket. It was so soft it had conformed to the shape of her hip. "What if it's that or nothing?"

He watched a young kid with a bleached blond forelock skateboard along the street, weaving in and out a group of women who didn't break stride or conversation. "So's I said..." went the conversation in loud Queens accents. "Then this skeevo said..."

Kit waited until they passed before answering. "I'd choose friendship." He gave Sabrina a sly-dog look, the blue of his irises almost incandescent in the filtered sunshine. "But only until I'd worked out a way to seduce you."

While his open "like" of her was flattering, it was the underlying heat that made her heart beat faster. She wanted him more than any other man she'd ever known—biblically, intellectually, emotionally. All of it. She wanted him on a level she couldn't even name, it was so intrinsic. If she'd been the old Sabrina, she'd get on him right there on the stoop. Instead she sighed deeply, withdrew the candy bar and started stuffing it into her face before it was completely unwrapped.

Kit watched her, contemplative and then amused when she sucked melted chocolate off her fingers and licked the torn silver paper. "With chocolate," he said, dabbing a corner of his napkin at a smear on her chin. "I'd seduce you with chocolate."

Sabrina licked her lips.

"FAVORITE MOVIE," Kit said a couple of days later from behind the wheel of a borrowed car. They were on their way to the West Side's passenger ship terminal to pick up Sabrina's parents.

No doubt about it, Kit thought. This platonic thing was for the birds. It was obvious what was meant to happen between them—the *opposite* of platonic—but Sabrina was sticking to her "pact" with Mackenzie. He was willing to bide his time, even if waiting drew out the inevitable. Spending extra time together didn't *have* to entail a serious involvement. Not with Sabrina. He might be enamored, but she'd been damn straight about not being a forever kind of girl. After she was out of his system, he could get back on track with his original plan to settle down.

Yeah, sure. Maybe if he kept telling himself that, he'd start to believe it.

Meanwhile, if they had to be friends first, he could manage. But they'd better get to know each other fast and be done with it before it *did* become complicated. Hence his questions.

"Hmm." Sabrina was thinking. "I guess my favorite is *Aliens*."

Unusual pick. "Favorite TV show," he said.

"I don't watch much TV."

"When you were a kid."

"Ah. Well...*Scooby Doo* and Wonder Woman. I wanted to kick butt."

"Which explains *Aliens*," he murmured. "Song?"

"I guess it would have to be 'Criminal' by Fiona Apple. Because I'm a bad, bad girl."

"Favorite foreign country."

"Mexico. And you? France, I'll bet."

"Right. Favorite state."

"Denial."

"You don't seem that type. You're too outspoken."

"I was being glib."

He shook his head. "Favorite state."

"Ecstasy." She gave an unconsciously sexy catlike stretch, pulling the seat belt taut between her breasts. Her nipples stood out like tiny buttons.

Had to be unconscious, he thought, breathing hard through his nose. Maybe innate. Given their platonic state, she couldn't be trying to rev him up on purpose. That would be cruel.

He grunted. "Coulda fooled me."

She grinned. "Hey, big guy, just because *you're* not getting it..."

A hot spurt of jealousy seared his gut, as if the chili pepper on her shoulder was real and he'd just bitten into her. Dammit. There went his reassurances. He *already* cared too much. No warning, no time to change his mind—she was just there, an important part of his life.

"Who?" he said through his teeth, letting out a low growl and pretending it was over the traffic snarl created by the Lincoln Tunnel commuters. Sabrina wasn't seeing anyone at Decadence, he knew that. She was a frequent topic of lusty conversation in the kitchen, but he was sure that none of the guys had actually gotten anywhere with her.

"I have a life outside of work, you know."

Yeah, he knew. He'd been trying to fill it at every opportunity. Volunteering to meet the parents wasn't normally his idea of the perfect day off.

"When?" he barked.

"When, what?"

With an effort, he toned it down from jealous boyfriend to concerned buddy. "When are you seeing these other guys?" Prowling the dance clubs after dark, he thought. Another jalapeño flamed his intestines. His forehead was sweating. And the window on the driver's side wouldn't open.

"I was teasing, Kit."

"Oh."

"Jeez."

"Um, sorry." In the Navy, he'd learned to channel his hothead temper into physical activity. After that, cooking had soothed him. In fact, cooking had made him so mellow, it had been a long time since he'd gotten this steamed up. Time to start running again, he thought. Maybe find a hockey league where body slams were acceptable behavior. If Sabrina kept putting him off, he'd need to blow off a lot of pent-up energy. Till then, he ought to wear a warning label: *Contents under pressure.*

"I didn't forget," he grumbled. "We're *friends.*"

"Well, be prepared for my mom and dad to assume otherwise. You know parents."

Charlie and Nicole Bliss were returning today from a honeymoon cruise. Kit had called in a favor and borrowed a car for the afternoon, making him, as Sabrina had put it—much to his chagrin—the best friend in the whole wide world. They were to meet the Blisses at the pier and drive them to their house in Scarsdale. He calculated that the outing was as good as packing a month's worth of friendly bonding into one day, topped off by the whole "meet the parents" deal. Not that he harbored any ulterior motives....

"I'll let *you* explain," he said. "You can give them your platonic lecture."

Sabrina scoffed. "They'll never believe it, not coming from me."

His fingers tightened on the steering wheel. She was open about her previous experience with what sounded like a constant rotation of boyfriends, which was fine, just fine, with him. He didn't care for coyness or double standards. So what was his problem?

At gut level, he knew: He wanted to be the *only* man in her life.

Her one and only.

Present tense, he tried to tell himself even though it was clearly useless. Hot obsessions never lasted, people said. They were supposed to burn out fast.

There was a break in traffic, so he took advantage and turned west toward the river. Suddenly the bustling harbor appeared between buildings. Sabrina leaned forward, excitedly pointing toward a cruise ship towering through the haze. "I've never been to the piers before. Where do we park? This place is a madhouse. We'll never find my mom and dad."

"They come off the ship in order, and there's a designated area for luggage dispersal."

She threw him an impressed glance.

"I read the directions," he said.

"Oh, yeah. I didn't." She flipped through the map and instructions Mackenzie had downloaded off the Internet and plotted in yellow highlighter as if she expected Sabrina to screw up otherwise. The proper terminal was marked with a big red X.

"Dear Mackenzie," Sabrina said with an exasperated sigh.

"Why didn't she come with us?"

"Something about an emergency shipment of jawbreakers. She'll be at the house later." Sabrina twined hair around her finger, gazing out her open window as he searched for parking along Twelfth Avenue. They ended up having to buy a ticket and use one of the paid-parking lots.

The dead-fish odor of the river was strong, mixed with the smells of hot pavement and wet wood. The palatial cruise ships gleamed, floating hotels temporarily docked at the wide piers. In the distance skeletal cranes hovered, unloading pallets and crates from a few of the working-class ships. The scene was far removed from an upscale restaurant kitchen in Tribeca, but just as familiar to Kit. The sailboats skidding across the water gave him a charge, reminding him that he missed the rolling decks and endless horizon. Manhattan was made up of so many gray canyons rushing with crowds that it could be easy to forget they lived on an island with open access to the sea.

Sabrina wasn't as absorbed by the harbor activity. She turned to him with a wry smile. "Are you ready for a family affair?"

A three-masted schooner had caught his eye. "Uh-huh."

"There's that enthusiasm I love."

"I'm here, right? That alone ought to earn me big points."

She pulled back, her face shadowed. "You volunteered. I didn't ask—"

"I know that." She didn't have to ask. Men were always eager to help women like her. Only a saint wouldn't take advantage.

He winced, realizing how rude he was being. "I shouldn't have said that." But it was regrettably true. He was angling for points. He wanted to get her out of his system—or maybe send her deeper—and the annoying just-friends stance she'd taken was not working for him.

She glared.

"Look, I'm sorry," he blurted. "Family stuff makes me uncomfortable. I don't know how to behave."

"How come?"

"I told you. It's all strange to me. I didn't have a family."

She softened. "You mentioned an aunt and uncle...."

"Right. But they considered themselves my guardians, not my family."

Sabrina looked as if she wanted to ask more questions, but he'd already said enough. He wasn't going to put on a poor-pitiful-orphan act, not even to score points. No way.

"Let's go," he said. "I'll try to behave right."

"Good," she answered with her usual tartness. "Because God knows one of us has to."

A COUPLE OF HOURS LATER, they'd arrived at the Bliss family home in Scarsdale. Kit was unloading blue-tagged luggage from the trunk and keeping an eye on Sabrina. She'd gone into a strange funk when her dad had started giving directions to the house. Kit didn't know why.

She stood in the driveway, staring at the house, not moving.

"It's a surprise for you and Mackenzie," Nicole Bliss said as she wrapped an arm around her daughter. "We thought you'd be pleased. Aren't you pleased, honey?"

"I'm stunned."

"What's the deal?" Kit asked sotto voce to Charlie when he came to heft a suitcase. Charlie Bliss looked like Sabrina's father should look: tall, bony, with crimped sandy-colored hair that was long on the sides and extremely sparse on top. He wore sandals and shorts with a wrinkled cotton batik shirt and wooden beads around his neck that gave him the air of an aging hippie.

"We bought back the old family home." Charlie's bleached eyebrows worked up and down his high forehead as he alternately smiled at Kit, then frowned worriedly at Sabrina. "It's the one we sold when we got divorced. Our girls never got over that, so Nicole and I are making amends." He sighed. "But Sabrina doesn't look so happy."

Nicole urged her daughter closer to the classic white two-story Federal-style house. "What do you think? Isn't this nice? It looks almost the same, doesn't it? I don't understand why you're not jumping for joy. We did this for you girls."

"It looks smaller," Sabrina said.

Charlie chuckled. "You just got bigger, Breen."

"I can't believe..."

"We're together again, all of us," Nicole said, beaming at her husband as he took her hand.

Sabrina looked at them oddly, then glanced back at Kit. "Help," she mouthed.

He didn't know why she was so stricken. The house was storybook perfect, and she had both parents hovering, going on about the good times they'd all have now that they were married again. If it had been him, he'd have—

Kit shook his head. It was senseless to put himself in her place. He wasn't ever going to have that, not from a child's perspective. His mom and dad had been nice people, by all reports. Regular folks. Mary Ann and David Rex, a schoolteacher and a business administrator. Kit had memories of going to church, playing ball with his dad in the backyard, opening presents on Christmas morning, but they were faded and unreal, like old photographs of strangers he'd met only once. After he'd been sent to live with his mother's sister and her husband and had started acting out, they'd sent him off to a weasely psychologist who'd said Kit was repressing his memories, but then the man had tried to get him to role play with dolls and he'd refused to go back. He'd been almost nine years old.

Damn if it hadn't taken twenty-five years and Ma'am's death to make him see that if he wanted to heal the past, he'd have to create his own family. He could be the kind of father his own might have been, if they'd had the chance. But he'd better do it with a woman who believed, who'd stick.

Not Sabrina.

The thought gave him an unpleasant jolt.

"Enter, enter." Charlie had unlocked the door and was ushering the women inside. "Leave the luggage and come join us, young man. This is an event."

"Everything's an event with you, Dad." Sabrina stopped short and wrapped her arms around herself. "Wow. This place really hasn't changed. They still have the Laura Ashley wallpaper." Pale yellow roses climbed the walls of the foyer.

Charlie flicked the light switch and a small crystal chandelier came to life. "And how about that—we have electricity."

Kit set the suitcases by the door, impressed with the Bliss home. The house belonging to his aunt's husband had been about this size, but as cold and unfriendly as its owners. Ma'am's house was a modest cottage with a cheap, home-built addition that had been slanting toward the outside wall before her husband had nailed the last board. Three foster sons had shared the extra bedroom in Kit's day. The cheap aluminum window screen screeched when he sneaked in and out at night, and the carpets were always smudged with dirt, but the place was a palace in his memory. One of Ma'am's married daughters with kids of her own lived there now.

"I planned for our furniture to be delivered while we were gone. Each room had a placement chart for the movers...." Nicole was flipping lights as she walked from room to room, her voice fading in and out. She circled around and reentered the sparsely furnished living room from the opposite direction. "They didn't do badly, but we'll still need to rearrange some of this. And hang pictures and put out my mother's china, of course."

"Not now, sweetheart." Charlie threw himself onto the sofa. "I'm exhausted."

His wife leaned over the sofa from behind and draped her arms around his shoulders. "You can't be that tired. We've just returned from a lengthy vacation." Her tone was sweet and coaxing, but with a slight edge.

Sabrina and Kit watched from the open doorway. He could feel her tense up beside him. She'd explained that her parents had been remarried two months ago, but had left some time later on their honeymoon. They'd been in touch by phone a couple of times, keeping tabs on their daughters.

Charlie patted Nicole's arm. "All in due time."

"You know I can't rest if my things are out of place."

"You're an annoying perfectionist," he said with an affectionate squeeze. "Have you forgotten we have company?"

"So we do." Nicole straightened. "The furnishings can wait. Let's sit down and get to know each other. Kit?" She motioned to an armchair. "Sabrina?"

Sabrina exhaled and went to sit beside her parents. With all three of them lined up, Kit felt as if he were facing a firing squad. Except that Sabrina wasn't paying much attention to him and her father was so genial and relaxed he'd never pull the trigger.

Nicole Bliss might. Despite the newlywed's long, lazy vacation, she was firing on target, her sharp gaze zipping from here to there, several beats ahead of the conversation. She was short and quite plump, with neat blond hair frosted with silver. Her casual cruise-wear looked bleached, starched and steam-pressed. She reminded Kit of one of his Navy commanders, Hal "Iron Eyes" Erwin, who'd once found Kit in the galley making cream puffs and had sworn he'd turn Kit into a proper sailor, sans apron, or retire his commission.

Mrs. Bliss might like to know that Kit was a pastry chef and old Iron Eyes was playing miniature golf in Boca Raton.

"Kit?" Nicole's smile was friendly and interested, but he could see the steel underneath. "What is that short for?"

"Kristoffer."

"Ah, Kristoffer Rex. A good name. So you're a chef, Kristoffer? I'd never have believed that it would be Sabrina who'd bring home a chef. Mackenzie, yes."

Charlie stifled a yawn. "Mackenzie brought home a lawyer, Nic, my dear. You heartily approved of Jason Dole."

"You *approved?*" Sabrina's voice escalated with irony.

"Indeed I did." Nicole pinched Sabrina's mouth into a moue, making her own kissy face in return. She waggled her head. "Your sister believes in the proprieties. She cares about her parents' opinions. She relies on our good judgment. You might try it."

Sabrina's squashed lips moved. "Isn't it too bad that Mackenzie dumped Jason, then?"

Nicole threw up her hands. "I don't know what is going on with you girls! Mackenzie quitting her job, you taking yet another new one—it's as if you're doing this just to make me crazy."

Sabrina worked her jaw. "It was your very unexpected wedding. You inspired us."

"She has you there, Nic," Charlie mumbled.

"Your father and I knew exactly what were we were doing. But as for you girls..." Nicole shook her head. "I was so sure that Mackenzie would marry Jason and I'd finally have my grandchildren."

"Well, there's Kit," Sabrina said with an innocent face. "I brought him by."

Oh, thanks, he thought, even as his hopes gave a leap.

"As if I'm fooled by that." Nicole returned her gaze to Kit. "So, Kristoffer." She scanned him head to toe. He briefly regretted the old running shoes, frayed jeans and Hobie Cat T-shirt, his customary day-off ensemble. A haircut wouldn't have been out of order, but at least the length hid his earring. And he had remembered to shave.

"Where are you from?" she asked.

"A small town in Ohio, originally. But I've lived all over."

"What do your parents do?"

Sabrina opened her mouth to interrupt, then closed it.

Kit had to answer. "Nothing. They're dead."

"I'm sorry," Nicole said, her expression sincerely distressed.

"Sure. No problem. Happened when I was eight-and-a-half. I barely remember."

Sabrina interjected. "Mom, Kit's a friend from work. He came along as chauffeur, not to be subjected to the third degree. Thank him nicely and offer him a drink."

"Of course. Although I'm afraid the refrigerator hasn't been stocked. We have water, and if Charlie can find the contents of the bar in one of these boxes, there may be liquor." Nicole bounced up. "Charlie?"

Charlie's mouth hung open, his head tilted onto the back cushion of the sofa. He let out a wheezing snore.

"Lazy," Nicole said. She reached for him, and for a second Kit thought she meant to shake him awake, but instead she gently closed his mouth and gave his bald head a pat. "Let's go into the kitchen," she whispered.

Sabrina blinked. She glanced at Kit and caught him studying her, so she threw out a little shrug and a care-free grin.

He wasn't fooled. Her parents were coloring outside the lines and she hadn't expected that.

As they crossed the foyer toward the kitchen, a ve-hicle drove up. Nicole perked. "That must be Macken-zie." She ran in quick, small steps to throw open the front door, squealing with excitement. "Kenzie, you made it. Surprise!"

Mackenzie was getting out of a cab. "Is this a joke? What are you doing in our old house?"

Nicole tottered out onto the brick steps in her high-heeled sandals. "We bought it!"

Sabrina caught Kit's hand. "Come on, let's make a getaway."

"We can't leave—"

She tugged him toward the staircase. "We're not leaving, just taking a reprieve. I want to see what's become of my old bedroom."

6

"YOU'RE GOING to get me in trouble," Kit joked as he followed her up the steps.

"Like that's new to you." The previous occupants had painted the upstairs hallway a hideous shade of purple and had hung a Chinese lantern over the light fixture. The place looked like a massage parlor. She was betting her mom would have her dad painting at sunrise the next morning.

Kit touched the dangling fringe of the lantern. "Interesting decor."

"Not my mother's. She's a proper suburbanite with a white tile bathroom and ironed sheets." Sabrina flicked a glance over her shoulder. "New sheets, of course."

"Forget about the sheets. I'd take you on a bed of nails if that was my only option."

"How romantic." She'd meant to be sarcastic, but her voice wobbled. Maybe Kit hadn't heard it.

He came closer, sliding his palm over her hip. "A bed of clover," he said, soft and coaxing.

"Allergies," she lied.

"Umm." He lifted her hair and kissed her neck, behind her ear. "A bed of roses."

She swallowed. "Thorns."

"A bed of spices."

"One giant sneeze would take care of that."

"You have no romance in your soul." He had kissed a necklace across her throat. She'd wear it forever.

"I'm pragmatic about these things."

"Pragmatic *and* platonic. A deadly combination." Kit had stopped kissing her.

She wanted to tell him to start again. Instead she reached for the doorknob to her old bedroom. She hadn't seen it since she was thirteen.

"This was me." The door swung open to a square room filled with exercise equipment. The walls were gray, the crown moldings white. Fresh paint. New carpet covered the old wooden floorboards.

"Now I know why you're so toned," Kit joked.

"They've turned it into a workout room."

"What did you expect? Horse posters?"

"I don't know. Maybe a guest room...." She walked around, touching the equipment. Her father was a runner, but he hated being cooped up, staring at walls while he exercised. This had to be her mother's doing. She was always planning to exercise and diet—making charts, listing menus. The failure to follow through was her greatest area of weakness, and Sabrina had been glad for it. After the divorce, the best times with her mom had been Sundays when the latest diet was an obvious failure and all three of them would go together to buy junk food before the new diet started on Monday. Mackenzie would come back with a bagful of penny candy; Sabrina chose barbecue potato chips; their mother consumed chocolate in mass quantities.

Chocolate. The lonely woman's solace.

"Why are you smiling?" Kit asked.

"I'm thinking that Mackenzie's right again."

"About what?"

"Oh...girl stuff." She approached him, running her hands over his T-shirt. His body was hard beneath it. "Got any chocolate on you?"

"No-o-o. But if you're looking for oral gratification..."

She held her face near his. She *did* have willpower. "You know we can't kiss. We're platonic."

"Who said anything about kissing?"

"Wicked! But I can't do that in the bedroom where I used to cut paper dolls and sing bubblegum pop."

"I can. I could." His cheek brushed hers. His lips moved, not quite touching. "Mmm...I would."

Crazy. She was having trouble breathing. "Would you?"

"Would you let me?" He put his hand on her rib cage, beneath her shirt. Pleasure burned from his fingertips. Her skin twitched. She always came alive under his touch.

"You already know I'm a bad, bad girl."

"Not here. In this room, you were a sweet child." His head ducked, trailing kisses down the center of her chest. He pinched the hem and V-neck of her crop top together, knotting them between his fingers so only her breasts remained covered. "You played with paper dolls. You dreamed about pony rides."

Ride me, she thought. *Let me ride you. Just for a day, a night, one perfect moment.*

But she'd promised. She'd made a commitment.

Had she ever kept a commitment? Not since...

She moaned. Kit's fingers were on her breasts, rubbing across her nipples, his teeth biting her top, dragging it higher. She was exposed. Not for long. His open mouth covered her, swallowed her, in deep pleasure, deep need.

She cradled his head, her body curving to sag against him. He sat on a workout bench, his arms twined around her rump, his hot mouth working her breast, sucking...sucking...

"*Oh,*" she cried. A wave of pure sensation rolled through her. Her back arched. Her shoulders hunched, offering him more. *More.* She always wanted more. "Ahhh."

"Sabrin-a-a?"

Her mother's voice cut through the haze of pleasure. Sabrina pushed Kit away, stumbling back on wooden feet as she jerked her top down, covering her wet breasts. She crossed her arms over them, holding in the stark, mindless passion. She'd lost herself. He'd barely begun and she was gone.

"Sabrina?" Her mother was getting closer. "Are you up here, honey?"

She glanced at Kit. He was still down on one knee, panting like a runner after a hard race.

"Sabrina." Sharper, now.

"In here, Mom."

Kit rose, but then sat abruptly on the weight bench.

The door opened. "You found my new workout room. Isn't it impressive? I wanted to get off to a fast start, so I hired painters to come in and redo the room while we were gone." Nicole looked around with pleasure. Her gaze landed on Kit. "Kristoffer—have you been lifting weights?"

"Uh, yeah," he said. "Bench pressing."

Arms still folded, Sabrina brushed her fingernails

across her collarbone. Anywhere his mouth had been, she tingled. "Yeah, Kit was showing off for me."

"Hmm. Has Kristoffer met Mackenzie?" Nicole gestured to her younger daughter, hovering in the doorway.

"Yes, he has. She's been to the restaurant." Sabrina waved a hello to Mackenzie, wondering if their mother was hoping to strike a match now that Mr. Dull was out of the picture. There was a hopeful air about her, and she'd claimed to have finally given up on Sabrina making a proper marriage. If so, Sabrina could only blame herself for insisting that Kit was strictly a friend.

A friend who'd just gone up her shirt. A friend who'd gotten so far under her skin that she had to carry more chocolate than the Easter Bunny in order to stave him off.

"Hey, Kit."

"Hey, Mackenzie."

"Don't lift too much weight."

"One hundred and twenty pounds ought to do it," he said, appraising Sabrina.

Nicole tittered, ignorant of the undercurrents. "There's something about a muscular man." She looked at her daughters. "Your father—" She shook her head. "It's never going to happen."

"You can't change him, not even with a couple thousand dollars of exercise equipment," Sabrina said, feeling especially prickly between her confusion about what she should do with Kit and the strangeness of being back in the old family home. She had to admit that so far, her remarried parents seemed to have found a balance that worked for them.

Nicole laughed gaily. "The room's not for Charlie.

It's for me. I probably gained fifteen pounds on our cruise. Oh, the food! The twenty-four-hour buffets! It was incredible.''

"I can't wait to hear all about the cruise, Mom.'' Mackenzie always smoothed over the rough spots. "But let's go take a peek into my old bedroom, okay?''

"At least yours won't be an exercise room,'' Sabrina said.

Her mother stopped short. "Why, darling, what did you expect? If you remember, you stripped your bedroom bare the day we moved out.'' She looked to Kit, explaining. "The poor girl hated moving. She was so mad at me that she cut off her nose to spite her face. Every possession went in the trash. I had to fish out a few of her clothes so she'd have something to wear to school.''

"Oh, please, Mom.'' Sabrina set her hands on her hips. Her face was flushed. "Don't bring that up. I admit it—I was a horrible, terrible, temperamental kid.''

"You were hurt. Moving was another upheaval. Your dad and I understood.'' Nicole leaned in closer to pat Sabrina's cheek. It seemed like a comforting gesture until her mother added in a whisper, "I think you're cold, Breen. Go put on one of my sweaters if you don't want Kristoffer to notice.''

Nicole swept Mackenzie out of the room. Sabrina put her face in her hands with an exasperated laugh. "Ugh. That was fun. My mother noticing my nipples and all.''

Kit laughed. "No comment.''

She eyed him. "It was a good thing we were interrupted or I might have—'' She stopped, unlike before.

"*We* might have,'' Kit said, approaching her.

She took off for the door.

"Would that have been so bad?" he called after her.

No, it wouldn't. And that was what scared her. With other men, she was in charge. She could pick and choose. Rarely were there hurt feelings—at least not that she knew of. Falling in love with Kit was giving her a new perspective.

She paused with her hand on the edge of the door. "Kit, this is only a flirtation, isn't it?"

His hesitation was fractional. "Sure."

Her heart dropped. "Are you saying that because you know I want you to?"

How was she going to tell him she'd changed her mind? That Mackenzie's little plan was working and he'd gained true boyfriend potential? Her being serious wasn't what he'd bargained for. She was the original good-time girl.

"Probably," he admitted.

"Oh. Well." She wasn't sure where that put them. "Do you mean that you want more from me than a few little kisses, or that—that—" She faltered because she couldn't say it. He'd be scared off if she admitted to falling in love.

Maybe she wasn't. Maybe it was just the chocolate.

"I've told you what I want, but I don't mind saying it again so we're straight." He came up close beside her—aggressive and substantially male. Another wave of pure lust swept through her. Except it wasn't really pure, not anymore. It carried far too much significance for a wherever-the-wind-blows girl like her.

"I want you naked in my bed," Kit said in his deepest, most shivery voice. "I want you screaming my name when you come."

That was good. She could handle that.

"I want you to think only of me."

Umm. Getting mighty possessive, there.

"Because I think only of you."

She searched his face. He was serious. Her hopes rose again, but she waited, wondering if there was a "...for now" coming. Wondering how that had come to matter so fast.

"You make me so damn hungry," Kit said, and kissed her with an undeniably hot, hungry mouth.

"Well, my goodness," her mother said from the purple hallway. "Is this what they call 'just friends' nowadays?"

Sabrina didn't answer. She was otherwise occupied.

MACKENZIE'S OLD BEDROOM was now a guest room, fairly anonymous except that their mother had kept the same bed frame and dresser, so at least it was a bit similar to what it had once been. Nicole left them to go and order in a late lunch from the deli, and Mackenzie started looking through unpacked cartons. She found a box of her old mementos in the closet. There weren't any for Sabrina, of course. That was her own fault.

"You kept nothing?" Kit asked her as Mackenzie cooed over stuffed animals. "Really?"

Sabrina picked up a finger painting. "It all went in the trash. I was ruthless."

She lied. She'd shoved her bronze horse statuette into her backpack, along with a diary and her favorite pair of jeans.

"So that was when you learned to travel light."

"After the divorce, Mackenzie and I were shuttled between houses. Shared custody. If I hadn't learned to carry all my belongings in a backpack, there would have always have been an item left behind."

Mackenzie chimed in. "Our dad's apartment was a typical messy bachelor pad. I lost a history book there once and never did find it."

"At least you had a home," Kit blurted.

Sabrina fixed her gaze on him. "Don't you remember anything of yours?"

He closed his eyes for a moment. "Very little."

"He's an orphan," Sabrina told Mackenzie. The mood in the room dropped, but then Sabrina gave a cheeky grin, determined not to wallow in depression. It was easier to shrug off the bad times when you had fun with them. "The worst I can say is that once my dad forgot me at soccer practice in the rain."

Kit wasn't impressed. "That's not so bad."

"Can you top it?"

"I'm trying to remember." He squinted one eye. "My aunt gave me a copy of *David Copperfield* and a year's supply of underwear and socks at our first Christmas together. My only presents."

Sabrina made a face at him, trying not to show that she was pleased he'd opened up a little about his past. "You're kidding about the book."

His eyes sparkled. "It might have been a comic book."

Mackenzie piped up as she shoved aside her box and reached into the closet for another. "Well, I once got a tube of Clearasil in my Christmas stocking."

"*Mother*," Sabrina said as they looked at each other and laughed.

"Hey," Mackenzie said a few seconds later. "There's a box in here with your name on it, Sabrina."

"Must be something from the other house."

Mackenzie dragged it out. "Open it and see."

Sabrina plopped down on the carpet beside the box and pried up the flaps. She pawed through a bunch of old tapes and tacky jewelry. "Yeah, it's just teenage junk." At the bottom was a stack of papers. She hoped her mother hadn't saved math tests and book reports on *Hamlet* to make up for the lack of other mementos.

"What's that?" Kit said, coming closer.

"Some of my old drawings." Sabrina paged through them, lingering over a construction paper turkey. "This is from kindergarten. I thought I threw this away in the great purge."

Mackenzie sat on the edge of the bed and reached into the box. "Here's a packet of *Little House on the Prairie* paper dolls. Worse for the wear. Why'd you rip Ma Ingalls in half?"

"But I did that when I threw—" Sabrina stopped. "Mom must have fished them out of the trash and saved them. How strange."

Mackenzie nudged her. "It was a very sweet thing to do."

"I guess so." Sabrina looked up at Kit. He was examining one of her doodles—misshapen horses galloped across a creased, wrinkled sheet of drawing paper. She cleared her throat. "I guess I underestimated Mom. I thought she didn't give a hoot about this stuff."

"Of course she did, Breen. You were just too fierce to confront. She didn't want to upset you even more."

Kit didn't say a word as he knelt down and picked up a butterfly painting. But there was a look in his eyes...

"Let's put this back," Sabrina said, dumping everything into the box before the congestion in her throat rose higher. She was *not* the sentimental type, except when it came to her grandmother's diamond ring. That was the only exception allowed, and even then when it came right down to it...

She'd rather have Kit.

"Can I keep this one?" he asked, taking the horse drawing over to the window, where he sat on the sill, gazing first at the drawing and then looking at Sabrina with an intensity that gave her the willies.

"Whatever," she said, suppressing a shiver.

"Here's your prom crown," Mackenzie announced, holding up a rhinestone circlet.

Sabrina snatched it away, dropped it in the box and shoved the whole shebang into the closet. "Enough with the memories."

Kit raised his brows. "You were the prom queen?"

"It was a joke. Becky O'Connor should have won. She was a cheerleader with school spirit. She dated the quarterback. I dated—I forget."

Mackenzie hadn't. "You went to the prom with that guy that Dad hated because he was so cocky—Alex somebody. He was from one of Westchester's grand old families. Went to Yale, drove a silver Lexus." She looked at Kit, almost like a warning. "He was crazy about her."

Kit nodded. "Yeah, I know the feeling."

"I dumped the guy," Sabrina said, a shade too loudly. "He got so serious and—" she shuddered "—clingy."

"Oh, boy," Mackenzie said. "The kiss of death." She glanced again at Kit. "I hope you don't have marriage plans."

He hesitated a beat too long, clearly measuring his response. "Not quite yet."

Sabrina felt as though an electric wire had been inserted in her spine. She was hot and then cold, shocked and then stricken with questions. Too many questions. She wasn't into analysis. She didn't like to dwell on the reasons for her actions. Leap, Don't Look, was her motto.

But she wanted to know. Was Kit saying he might have plans? Were they with her? Or after her?

After, she thought. Of course. He had no reason to believe that she wanted more from him than a fling.

And she did.

She wanted more, and more, and more.

With Kit, there could never be enough.

But marriage? That was absurd. Maybe they could try dating first. A few casual dates didn't have to lead anywhere serious, even though Mackenzie was hoping it would.

"I need a little sweet something," she announced.

Mackenzie started. "You mean...?"

Sabrina nodded, hoping her sister could see the desperation in her eyes. If she didn't get doped up with chocolate, and soon, she was going to say or do something regrettable. Not because of the pact. Because of Kit. Herself. And their impossible future.

Regardless of her attachment to the family engagement ring, she was *not* getting married. She'd rather award the ring to Mackenzie right now. She'd only known Kit for a couple of weeks, too soon for there to be anything between them but a basic animal attraction. The idea of marriage was ridiculous! Even more

ridiculous than thinking chocolate could cure hor-
niness.

But wasn't she supposed to go against her inclina-
tions and change her life?

"MARRIAGE IS WONDERFUL," Charlie announced over
their deli lunch on the brick patio behind the house.

Kit wasn't sure he was meant to be a part of this conversation, so he glanced around the backyard, looking
for distraction. The old vegetable patch Sabrina had
told him about had been resodded into blank, boring
lawn. Rhododendron bloomed beside a crowded patch
of bearded iris, but the peony and lilac bushes were
leggy and sadly neglected.

Nicole Bliss fed her recycled husband a spear of dill
pickle. "We're worried that we've given you girls the
wrong impression."

"If we could do it over again, we'd have stuck it out
the first time." Charlie crunched the pickle to the nub,
then kissed her fingertips with a smack. "Yes, my
love?"

They rubbed noses, making more kissy noises. Kit
was drawn to watch in spite of himself. Seeing the
Blisses together made the old, faded memories of his
parents nudge at the corners of his mind. He could *almost* remember...his dad in an apron...a barbecue in
the backyard....

Sabrina was picking at a roast beef on rye. When the
doorbell had rung, she'd galloped downstairs with Kit
and Mackenzie on her heels, grabbed the sandwich
bags from the delivery boy and rummaged through
them like a wild woman. Even though her mother had

protested, Sabrina had eaten dessert first—a giant iced brownie. She'd seemed slightly off ever since.

"Why are you looking so nervous?" Mackenzie whispered, loud enough for Kit to overhear even though she put down a large messy Reuben to tilt closer to Sabrina.

Sabrina spoke so softly Kit had to hold his breath to catch her words. "You can have the ring. I've got to get away from here."

The ring?

"Aren't you happy to see Mom and Dad getting along so well?"

"Oh, I am. But..." Sabrina stole a glance at Kit. He kept his expression neutral, not meeting her eyes. Finding the box of childhood keepsakes had seemed to throw her. Or maybe it was *him.* She was as wary as an untamed animal every time he got near.

"Don't give up now. You can stick it out." Mackenzie grinned and bit into her sandwich.

Sabrina stood, abruptly pushing back her chair. Kit halfway expected her to bolt, but instead she went over to envelope her parents in a bear hug. They were surprised, then delighted. She squeezed them even tighter. "Don't worry, you guys. Mackenzie and I are fine. Just fine. You did a wonderful job raising us. No regrets."

Mackenzie reached over to take her dad's hand. "Absolutely positively."

Kit watched them, feeling set apart but strangely involved. An image flashed in his mind's eye of himself in *Star Wars* pajamas, sitting between his parents on the couch while they watched TV....

Squished by the hug, Nicole let out a peep of protest.

She pulled away, straightening her striped top and tucking her hair behind her ears. "I appreciate the thought, Sabrina. But I must beg to differ. Neither of you seems capable of settling down—"

"Hah." Mackenzie crunched a potato chip. "I couldn't get any more settled."

"But you broke up with Jason while we were gone. And he was so perfect. There has to be a reason that you girls are holding back from marriage." She took Charlie's other hand. "We don't want it to be us. That would be a terrible legacy for our daughters."

Sabrina started to sidle away, but then she stopped. "It's not you—any of you. It's me. Hey, we all know it's me." She laughed, waving her hands. "Ms. Short Attention Span. Wings on my heels. Reckless. Irresponsible. Whatever you want to call it—"

"Now, Sabrina," Charlie said. "Don't you talk like that. I'm damn proud of both my daughters." He beamed around the table at each one in turn, including Kit in the expansive approval in a way that made him sit up a little straighter. "Here's Mackenzie, opening her own candy store. And Sabrina, with an apartment and a good job..." Charlie raised a can of soda. "And we're all here, together at the family house. I couldn't ask for more."

Filled with optimism even though Sabrina still looked like a deer caught in the headlights, Kit reached for his own can.

"To family," Charlie said.

"To family," the rest of them chorused, Kit the loudest of all.

7

"Why am I—" *pffffft* "—blowing up balloons?" Sabrina stopped to gasp for breath.

She, Kit and Mackenzie had driven back to the city together. After they'd dropped Mackenzie off at her apartment and left Kit's friend's car in a parking garage, they'd come to Decadence. It was closed on Mondays, but Kit said he wanted to get a head start on a special job and he needed an assistant. Then he'd given her a handful of balloons to inflate. Big deal.

Kit was busy running water into a double boiler and adjusting the flame on the massive industrial cookstove, so Sabrina blew up another balloon while she waited for his answer.

How strange it was, to be in the restaurant kitchen during off-hours. The stainless-steel surfaces gleamed, the pots hung untouched on the overhead rack. There was no sound except the humming of the glass-fronted industrial refrigerators. Most days, the chefs were already at work when she reported in. She'd never seen the place so quiet and clean. Even the large butcher-block worktable was completely uncluttered.

But she liked the noise and confusion better. On any given day, Parker would be making lewd jokes and Vijay would be blushing, shooting alarmed looks at Sabrina. She'd pretend she hadn't overheard, to save Vijay from defending what he imagined was her innocent virtue. Mario Alfieri, the executive chef, would be shouting at somebody—anybody. Even he admitted that he yelled because he cooked best when his passions were running on high. There'd probably be a delivery man at the back door, unloading fresh lobsters from Maine, or baskets heaped with brightly colored vegetables. The entire kitchen would be infused with cooking smells....

Tonight she had only Kit.

No distractions, except chocolate, which had grown old fast. She'd probably consumed so much of it she'd built up a resistance.

At that thought, Sabrina sucked in a huge breath, put another balloon to her lips and blew.

"Hold on," Kit said, abandoning the double boiler. "You're making them too big."

"Too big?" She tilted her head at the rounded pink balloon. "So you're saying size matters?"

"In this case, yes." He plucked the balloon from her fingers and, with his fingers squeezed on the end, deflated it by half.

"Whoa," she said. "Premature deflation."

Kit laughed in surprise, letting go of the balloon. It made a rude noise as it flew, zigzagging in a crazy pattern as the rest of the air was expelled. It fell to the floor near the island.

Sabrina got off her stool and picked it up. She waggled the stretched-out piece of rubber. "Aw. It's gone limp."

"Then I guess size no longer matters."

"Tell that to the lady balloons."

Kit motioned her over. "Get back here. Let me explain."

She climbed onto the stool. "Is this going to be about man inches?"

"Man inches?" he repeated in an I-shouldn't-be-asking way.

"You know, man inches. Twice as big as regular inches. Like how the fish they caught were this big." She spread her hands in the air. "Also applies to how much snow they shoveled. And especially the size of their—"

"Right. I get the idea."

He ignored her saucy smile while he stirred the chocolate before removing it from the heat. "This is not about man inches. It's about the recipe. We're making chocolate cups for tomorrow. If you blow up the balloons too big, we'll get chocolate bowls instead."

"If you say so..."

"Let me demonstrate." Kit took one of the balloons from the package, gave it a stretch, and neatly blew it into a small orb. He tied it off, holding it up for her inspection. "That's big enough. In *any* inches."

"Says you."

"I'm boss in the kitchen."

And the bedroom? she thought, wondering if he'd ever exaggerated his man inches.

"Blow," he commanded.

She laughed and selected a balloon. "Oh, man, you're really asking for it."

"Just blow." Smiling to himself, Kit stirred the chocolate that had melted in the top of the double boiler. He got out several baking sheets and lined them with sheets of parchment paper.

Sabrina blew until she had a headache. After seeing the deep look of longing in his eyes when he'd joined her family's toast, she was in a mood to give Kit anything he wanted.

"Now," he said, taking up a balloon, "let me demonstrate." He dipped the small balloon in the chocolate, coating it about halfway up. With deft turns of his wrist, he rotated the balloon so that the cooling chocolate formed a scalloped edge. He put the coated balloon on the parchment, holding it for a moment so that the excess chocolate pooled at the bottom, forming a sticky base. When he let go, the structure stayed in place.

"We'll pop the balloons after the chocolate's hardened, and *voilà*—we have chocolate cups. I'm going to fill them with chocolate-orange mousse, but they're good for a variety of fillings."

"Neat trick." She applauded. "Can I try?"

"Sure."

She moved next to him. Working beside Kit was beginning to feel natural. Not easy—she was too aware of his body—but *right.*

"Not too much chocolate," he coached when she dipped her first balloon. "Oh, wait. I forgot who I'm talking to—the chocolate queen."

Kit's chuckle, so low and manly, made her lose concentration. He took her hand in his, showing her how to manipulate the balloon so the liquid chocolate went where she wanted it to go. His palm was warm and his touch gentle. For just a second, she let her eyes drift shut while she imagined him manipulating her body in the same skilled way—lifting her breasts, curving his palms around them, squeezing and licking and twisting the tips between his lips, then turning her over and, oh my stars, starting all over again....

"And set it down," Kit said, guiding her arm to the pans.

She cocked her head this way and that, examining the cup while it hardened. "It's lopsided."

"That's okay. Perfection isn't necessary. Yours will look like a tulip with a missing petal."

She scooped a dollop of chocolate from the edge of the pan and sucked it off her finger. *Endorphins, don't fail me now.*

"Let me do another?"

Kit blinked. His eyes were opaque. "Uh, sure. We need to use up all the chocolate." Unfortunately, he moved off, trusting her to manage without his guidance. "You work on those and I'll start melting the white chocolate so we can make marbleized cups."

Sabrina soon got the hang of it and filled two pans with the tulip-shaped cups. Kit demonstrated a marbling technique with the white chocolate and they kept on working. The shells would be refrigerated overnight, ready to be filled for tomorrow's dessert of the day.

"Thanks for helping," he said when they were finishing up. "This has been an interesting day."

She apologized. "I shouldn't have put you through all that family drama, especially when you were so nice about borrowing the car and all."

"No," he said. "Don't think that. Meeting your family gave me a new perspective on you."

"Who says that's a good thing?" She shuddered. Was he going to dissect her psyche now? Ugh.

"You're lucky and you don't know it."

"I do know it, Kit. My parents weren't perfect, sure, but I'm not ungrateful and I'm not *that* screwed up, either. When I compare my childhood with yours—" Her voice caught.

"Hey, there. Don't get all sappy on me now."

She remembered how she'd teased him about being an orphan. "I hope you know I wasn't discounting your, um, unfortunate circumstances...."

He shook his head, smiling a little. "I like your irreverence."

"You ever read the Lemony Snicket books?" She bumped him with her elbow. "Poor little orphan."

"Poor little rich girl."

"Rich? You're kidding, right?"

"That house looked rich to me."

"Hmm, well, remember we left it after the divorce. Mom managed to keep us in Scarsdale, but we'd definitely dropped a level or two on the class scale."

"I'm strictly from working-class roots. To my aunt's humiliation. I think that was a big part of why she hated having me around—" Kit stopped. Frowned.

"Go on," Sabrina urged. This wasn't analyzing—it was being a good listener.

"I was sent to them when I was eight, after my mom and dad were killed in a car accident. I was in the back seat when it happened, but I've never been able to remember it. Traumatized, I guess. My aunt was my mother's sister, the only blood relative I had left, so she and her husband were more or less forced into taking me on. But she didn't know what to do with me. I made noise and messed up her fancy house and later I figured out that worst of all I was a reminder of her humble roots. My uncle didn't like me because he was a cold, miserly man who only put value on things, not people."

"But if you had this aunt and uncle, even if they were rotten people, how did you end up a foster child?"

"That was my fault. I wanted out, any way possible, so I got into more and more trouble as the years went by. Finally, when I was arrested after crashing a stolen car into the window of a pharmacy, they gave up and made me a ward of the court. I haven't seen them since."

"But you were, what—only fourteen?"

"That's right." Kit took a spoon and scraped it around the sides of the chocolate pan. He held it up toward her lips. "Can we change the subject now?"

Obediently, she swallowed the chocolate. Would its happy chemicals help with an aching heart?

He withdrew the spoon slowly, his gaze fixated on her lips. "You have a drop of chocolate at the corner of your mouth."

"Mmm." She puckered, waiting.

Kit's face came closer. His stubble grazed her chin as he leaned in and flicked his tongue at the chocolate. Her lips parted with unspoken invitation, but he drew back.

"Was there really any chocolate there?" she asked.

He grinned. "Do I need an excuse to kiss you?"

"You need permission."

"Then..." The sexual tension between them was so tangible it seemed to make the air shimmer. "May I?"

"You didn't use the secret word."

"Well, it's not *please*, so it must be..." His mouth hovered so near to hers she felt the vibrations of his throaty voice when he whispered, "*Chocolate?*"

She slid her arms around his shoulders. "How did you guess?"

"Because you taste—" he dropped small kisses on her mouth, three in a row "—like chocolate. And I'm—" he gave a rough, sexy purr and used his teeth and tongue on her lower lip "—a chocolate connoisseur." He pulled on her lip, nibbling, suckling, softly biting, dipping his tongue inside. She played passive for a little bit, enjoying the attention...and the feelings swirling inside her.

With his hands on her waist, Kit pressed closer. No worry about man inches there. His arousal was apparent—and wickedly tempting. She rocked against him, and one of his hands lowered to her bottom, squeezing her, urging her to continue. That rigid bar of flesh, so aggressively male and blatant about Kit's needs, sent a shivery, tingly response racing through her. She became moist, swollen...prepared. Her lips, moving now under his, asked him to deepen their kiss. He obliged with a bold, hungry thrust.

Sabrina moaned. She wasn't thinking about pacts or promises—she was thinking about making love. On the countertop. On the tile floor. On every table in the restaurant.

His right hand came up to cup her breast, opening and closing reflexively. "Let me taste you," he said, gripping the neckline of her cotton crop top. The straps slid off her shoulders. She nodded and he tugged, too hard because the top tore a little down the middle.

"Sorry," he said, but he wasn't in the least and neither was she. His mouth had locked on her nipple. The delicious shock of sensation made her melt and he held her up, his hands going to the back of her thighs as he boosted her onto the butcher block, one sweeping shove sending the pans of chocolate cups skidding over the surface like bumper cars. And his mouth hadn't let go of her breast—he was drawing it deeper into his mouth, shooting streaks of pleasure through her like lightning bolts.

He pushed against her. Her thighs opened wide to accommodate him. They were on a perfect level now—his erection hit the right spot, the hot, flowing center of her. She locked her ankles around his hips, panting and needy, half out of her mind, wanting to ride him until the sharp, dark, forbidden thrill had shattered. Not even the layers of their clothing was a deterrence. They only added an extra degree of friction.

The industrial refrigerators hummed. Her body sang. She was wrapped around Kit, clinging, rubbing. He sucked harder, thrust a hand down the front of her jeans. One touch, one flicker of his fingertip against the wet cotton of her thong and she went rigid. Flames licked out from her knotted nerve endings—she was too sensitive to be touched. "No! Oh, Kit. I'm—"

He touched her anyway. The fire became a liquid heat, spilling over her. Her thighs clamped around his waist, every muscle twitching in the series of hot, exploding spasms.

When it was over she dropped her head against his shoulder, moaning softly. "Umm. Yumm." There was more she needed to say, but her brain had broken into too many pieces to make sense.

Kit wasn't as relaxed as she. Under her cheek she felt the rapid rise and fall of his chest. Hot, panting breaths ruffled her hair. She lifted her head, rather dopily, and made a questioning sound.

Okay. They weren't finished—

He sucked in a gasp when she reached for his fly. "Uh, no," he said, disentangling from her. He took a couple of steps and leaned over the worktable, his chest still heaving. "Give me a minute."

"But I can—"

"Not here." His tousled head came up and she felt the full force of his eyes. "Let's go. My place is closer—"

She cleared her throat. Closed her thighs.

"Your place, then," he said gruffly, going up on one elbow. "I don't care." He stretched an arm across the butcher block, shackling her wrist, dragging her closer. His eyes drilled hers. "As long as I have you in a bed where I can properly sink myself into you."

Sweet mercy. She wanted that, too. Her body, as open and yearning as if he'd never stopped stroking her, was reacting merely to the words.

"Kit," she sighed, drawing out his name because she didn't know how to explain that she was turning him down.

He swore under his breath. So, he already knew.

She slid off the butcher block, so wrung-out she was limp. He still had her wrist, his fingertips felt almost bruising. "Kit," she crooned, draping herself along his bent form. "Of course we can make love...eventually."

His head dropped to the table with a thud. "What?" He'd gone hoarse.

"It's just that...I mean...we got carried away, right? And, um, well, I have this com—commitment to Mackenzie—"

He straightened, brushing her aside. "Mackenzie, *again?*"

"I told you about our pact." But not in whole. The entire explanation was a teeny bit embarrassing, seeing as how he'd just gotten her off and now she had to back out of what had been a pretty implicit promise. You didn't get a guy so riled up without meaning to give him some sort of...

Chocolate.

"Oh, look. We broke a few of the chocolate cups." The pans were off-kilter, with a number of the shells knocked over and several cracked into pieces. She sounded perky, like a sorority girl, but she was desperate. "Let's taste."

Kit was looking at her as if she'd gone nuts.

"Here you go." She pushed a piece of marbleized white-and-dark chocolate between his lips. He took it, apparently dazed by the sudden switch in subjects. She patted his shoulder. Man, it was like a boulder. Stood to reason—his nerves had to be stretched taut as a drum skin. "Have another piece. You'll feel better soon."

He swallowed. "It's going to take more than chocolate."

Maybe white chocolate didn't have the same chemical properties? She broke off a thick piece from the base of one of the pure chocolate cups and held it up to him. "Try this."

He brushed her hand aside. "I don't need chocolate."

"It has natural amphetamines, or something like that. I don't remember the technical terms, but Mackenzie explained it all to me. Chocolate will give you the same rush of good feelings as, um..."

She stopped. Kit's eyebrow was raised with a skepticism she couldn't deny. Especially after she'd experienced the real thing only a couple of minutes ago. Chocolate was good, but it couldn't hold an endorphin to the sheer, screaming ecstasy of a Kristoffer Rexbrand climax.

"WHAT HAPPENED THEN?" Mackenzie asked, looking at Sabrina from beneath clumps of wet, pinned-up hair. It was three days after the incident in the kitchen at Decadence, and Sabrina was still skittish when she got near Kit. He wasn't angry with her, exactly, but he was back to brooding—when he wasn't giving her long, lingering looks that made her feel as if she were standing over a steam grate with her dress blown up around her ears. And, unlike Marilyn, she didn't have on any panties.

"We went home," she said, fiddling with the hem of her skirt.

"You didn't—"

"No. We went to our own homes. Separately."

Mackenzie leaned back in the salon's retro pink Lucite chair. "Woooo. Hard to believe you passed up such a hot guy. The chocolate remedy must be working for you. Or else you *really* want that ring."

Sabrina would have laughed, because it hadn't been the chocolate, but she realized that almost everyone in the salon had been listening in on the conversation. The entire row of transparent pink-and-black chairs were tilted in their direction. Even the snobby stylists were eavesdropping.

Enough with the entertainment. Sabrina made a snipping motion at Costas Cartouche, the much-in-demand stylist whom she'd managed to get another appointment with, via Dominique. Mackenzie was nervous, so to distract her, Sabrina had launched into the tale of her latest choco-adventure with Kit—which would now be disseminated to chichi girlfriends and gay hairdressers all over the Upper East Side.

"Technically, you haven't broken the pact," Mackenzie said, not even noticing that Costas had begun to cut off her hair. Long hanks of it fell softly to the floor.

"Humping doesn't count?" Costas said in his pseudo-European accent. He had extremely short black hair, a Botoxed forehead and wore blue wrap-around sunglasses.

Heat shot into Sabrina's face. "Pleeeze! I am not a dog in need of behavior modification." But she *was* accustomed to her chocolate treats. And she had been rubbed almost raw.

She leaned against the pink tile counter ledge and crossed her legs.

"Does humping count?" called Costas, and got a chorus of replies from all over the upscale salon.

Sabrina buried her face in her hands. "Kill me now."

Costas leveled his silver scissors at her. They were attached to a beaded, leather-braided cord that hung around his neck, like a pair of old lady's sunglasses at Rockaway Beach. "She did not have sex with that man."

"I don't know if I can continue to hold you to this bet," Mackenzie said. "It's cruel and unusual punishment."

Costas snipped. "Absolutely."

Mackenzie looked in the mirror and let out a shriek. "My hair—it's gone!" She ran her fingertips over the shorn ends. "Good Lord. It's as short as a boy's."

"Don't panic," Sabrina said. "Costas knows what he's doing."

He was taking down the sections he'd pinned up and combing them over Mackenzie's startled face. "You need very short hair, sugar pie. You've got the curvy thing happening—" One hand shaped the air, then slapped his outthrust Pleather-clad rump. "A pixie cut will be delish in contrast to all that flagrant femininity." He tilted her chin up rather firmly. "Hold still."

The scissors went *snip, snip, snip.*

Mackenzie whimpered.

"You're going to look like a brand-new you," Sabrina encouraged.

"I liked the old me. She gave me no trouble."

"Gave you no fun, either."

Mackenzie squinted from behind her rapidly disappearing hair. "Seems to me that since you got nasty with Kit on a butcher block I should be able to keep to shoulder-length, at least."

Costas spun her chair. "Too late, sugar pie."

"Eep! I felt a breeze on the back of my neck," Mackenzie said in awe.

"And don't you feel lighter, too? You're dropping ten pounds, just from a haircut."

She elongated her neck, looking past Sabrina to the mirror. "You're right. I should have done this years ago."

Costas preened. "I'll have you, next," he said to Sabrina, staring in horror at the messy way she'd clipped her long hair up off her neck.

She shook her head. "This is Mackenzie's turn. Besides, I've tried short. I did the whole zip cut, bleached white thing when I was twenty."

"We could straighten it, at least. The *Felicity* show was canceled, sugar pie." *Snip, snip.*

Mackenzie let out another *eep*. "Watch the ears, huh?"

"I haven't drawn blood yet," Costas said airily. He was fingering through what remained of Mackenzie's hair, snipping off an eighth of an inch here and there. He stopped, looked in the mirror—at himself—and hissed. "Sssss. Except with my tongue."

"You tell it, sistah," said the neighboring stylist.

Sabrina winced. "When you speak of this—and you will—please be kind."

"Anything for a friend of Dominque's," Costas said. She didn't believe him for a New York minute.

Mackenzie was sent off to be fluffed dry and Sabrina was relegated to the waiting area. She watched Costas do the cheek air kiss with a teenager who had platinum blond, stick-straight hair, a cell phone glued to her ear, a Chinese symbol tattooed on her biceps and a yipping Pomeranian tucked in her Kate Spade bag. *Yawn.*

Sabrina flipped through copies of *W* and *Hamptons* magazine, finding a papparazzi shot of Dominique and Curt at a Maidstone charity event. Golfing for Genomes.

She had to look twice when Mackenzie came out. "Wow. Your hair is *short.*"

Mackenzie waggled her head, holding it high. "But my neck is long. Who'd have guessed?"

"You're beautiful! Costas was right—you've lost ten pounds of hair."

Mackenzie lowered her voice as she took Sabrina's

arm and drew her out of the salon. "Sounds like the kind of diet I could live with, but I just found out that Costas was actually referring to the lightening of my wallet. Do you have any idea how expensive he is?"

"But worth it?" They emerged from the glass doors onto Madison Avenue. The sky was blue. The air was almost pure—or at least breathable, without the heavy tar smell it would have later in the summer. A woman decked out in head-to-toe designer gear skimmed a glance over them, which snagged briefly, but approvingly, on Mackenzie's hair.

Mackenzie looked at her reflection in the shiny glass. The haircut had revealed the shape of her face, her graceful neck. She was trim and chic as never before, and the wonder of that showed in her expression. Sabrina's heart warmed. Her baby sister was all grown-up—stylish, savvy and soon to be outrageously successful.

Mackenzie nodded. "Yes, Costas was worth it."

"Costas Car-*touche*," Sabrina said with a silly giggle. "Did you know that Costas came to New York from Baltimore, not Europe? Dominique knew him when he was Bobby Cartman, doing freelance gigs out of the back of his van. They started out in modeling together. She says he once fried her hair so badly she had to have it all cut off. Then Linda Evangalista copied the cut and a sensation was born. Costas and Dominique still complain about not getting the credit for that."

Mackenzie turned away from the doors. "Well, I'm no skinny model, but I do look good if I say so myself."

"You look excellent."

"And just in time for my grand opening." She

peered at Sabrina as they walked to the Lexington train stop. "You're still coming?"

"Of course I am."

"With Kit?"

"Mmm."

"You have to! He agreed. And he doesn't look like the kind of man who'd back out."

"What if we can't keep our hands off each other?"

Mackenzie grinned as a blast of warm air from the steps that led down into the subway ruffled her newly fringed hair. "Then you lose the bet. I may get the ring, but you'll win Kit. That, dear sis, is what gamblers call a push."

Sabrina laughed, suddenly feeling lighthearted about the whole thing. She could win for losing! "Well, as long as he pushes me onto a bed, I'm ready to give it a go."

For a second she thought that Mackenzie was going to launch into a lecture about commitment and caring and all that crap, but instead she merely gave her cropped head a fond shake and skipped like a school-girl down the station steps.

8

"I CAN'T HELP FEELING that you're mad at me," Sabrina said from her favorite spot—the stool beside the stainless steel countertop of Kit's workstation. They were tucked out of the way of the big guns. Kit liked it that way. He could create in peace without being hassled by rampaging egos and entrée wars. Thanks to Sabrina, he now thought of her man-inch theory every time Parker boasted about the superior quality of his grilled swordfish.

She peered at him, looking very ladylike in her pearl earrings and pale blue dress. "*Are* you mad at me?"

"Nope."

She put her feet to the floor and slid partway off the stool. Her dress rode up an inch or two, revealing smooth honey-colored thighs. Sunbathing on her fire escape again. She'd discovered there was almost an hour of sunlight between buildings before the shadow of the water tower fell across her apartment.

For a couple of seconds, the noise level in the kitchen decreased by half. Then Sabrina stood and smoothed down her skirt. A cumulative sigh was expelled as the kitchen staff turned away and went back to work.

Kit slid his raspberry sauce off the fire two seconds before it would have been ruined. When Sabrina was around, he'd learned to be extravigilant.

"You don't talk to me the way you used to."

Had they ever talked? Kit wondered. Well, yeah, they had. More than he'd talked with any other woman. He'd damn near spilled his guts, and he wasn't sure he liked the feeling of her knowing what went on his head. Especially when she continued to make it clear that she wasn't going to stick around. It didn't take a feel-good pop psychology doctor to know that having another woman disappear from his life was the last thing Kit needed.

But for now Sabrina had become a friend. He liked her.

Except when he looked at her. Then he only wanted her. Wearing a skirt that short was grounds for ravishment.

"I'm working here," he said. "Quit bothering me." Had he added six eggs to the cake batter, or five?

"Well, you're going to have to talk to me. We need to go over your ideas for the dessert course of the IRO luncheon. Dominique's friend Daffy has been on my case. She wants something unique."

"How about a Saint Honoré cake?"

"I don't know what that is."

"A tower of cream puffs drizzled with caramel."

"Nah. I was thinking chocolate...."

"Chocolate again? Aren't you tired of chocolate?" He didn't look at her, but out of the corner of his eyes he could see her discomfort. Their make-out session in the kitchen stood between them like a blinking stoplight. Guess who was always slamming on the brakes?

"This isn't about me," guess-who said.

"No, it's about feeding two hundred socialites who think food is the enemy. Chocolate, it is. Maybe we should put chocolate in their drinks."

"Chocolate martinis? Good idea. I'll make a note of that." Sabrina rattled on. "We can serve the Decadence brownie, of course. But we need something grand for the center of the buffet table, something really eye-catching. Daffy also wants individual desserts to put on all the tables. Can I trust you to come up with a unique presentation?"

He was about to say, "That's my job," when he thought of a better idea.

"I'll experiment."

Sabrina hesitated. "O-kaaay."

"I haven't been able to let my creative side loose since the flaming Cherries Jubilee incident at the resort in Papeete."

"Oh."

He threw her a cheesy grin. "Don't worry. I won't set off the sprinklers this time."

"Now, Kit..."

"I could do an edible construction," he said, ruminating.

"We want unique, not gaudy. Something small and portable for the tables—like chocolates."

He waved a dismissive hand. "Chocolates. Eh."

"But I hear you make great hand-dipped chocolates. Charmaine was telling me you distributed them to all the employees at the holidays—"

"Nope, no good," he insisted. "Been there, dipped that. I'll start experimenting tonight at home. Maybe..." He stopped to search his mind for the worst dessert he'd ever tried. "*Akutaq.*"

Sabrina looked worried. Good. "Which is?"

"Eskimo ice cream. Made with moose fat, seal oil and salmonberries."

"Kit!"

"No?"

"Definitely no. Dominique's society gal pals would die."

"Never fear. I shall release my creativity and concoct—" he puffed up his chest and waved his hands, doing his best impression of an out-of-control chef "—a glorious work of art."

"Perhaps you should have a taste tester."

He squinted an eye at her. "You think?"

"One of your assistants?"

"I hate to make them work overtime. When my creative juices get flowing, I can be in the kitchen for hours." She frowned. "Experimenting," he added for emphasis. "With unique combinations, like pistachio and nutmeg."

"Don't forget, I have approval."

"Yes, boss."

"Maybe I should—uh, no, that's not a good idea."

"Hmm?"

She crossed her arms, trying to look stern and managerial. "Should I come by? To taste?"

"Hmm, yeah," he said as if he had to think about it. "That would be great. You can try the snickerdoodles while they're fresh."

"Snickerdoodles?" She backed out of the kitchen. "You'd better be joking, Rex."

He stirred the sauce. "See you tonight."

She made a face at him as she disappeared through the swinging door, but it was the hint of satisfaction underlying it that brought him up short. Suddenly he wasn't so sure about who was being played.

"Good work, man," Parker called across the kitchen.

Although Kit bowed to the smattering of applause, his mind was churning. Damn that Sabrina. She refused to stay in the box he'd first put her in, the one he'd mentally labeled: Fast Serve, No Reservations Required. Now that he'd met her family and seen behind her facade, his feelings were more complicated than ever. All he knew for sure was that the decision he'd made at Ma'am's graveside had been reinforced, not destroyed. But he still couldn't get a handle on how Sabrina would feel about his plan to build a family. Especially if she was at the center of it.

"So THIS is your place, huh?" Sabrina said as Kit let her inside. A brilliant conversational gambit.

Not a little of the blame had to go to Kit. He'd cultivated the sexy, stubbly, barefoot-in-drawstring-pants look to a fine art. His football jersey was the kind that was perforated by thousands of teeny-weeny holes. It was bleached and frayed, with a chunk torn away in the front, giving her a glimpse of the flat, hairy washboard that was his abdomen.

One look and she was melting like an Italian ice, puddling in her vintage Puma sneakers. She tugged her baggy khaki shorts an inch lower on her hips. "Do you have air?"

"It's not that hot since the sun went down, is it?"

"This apartment is roasting."

"I've had the stove on all evening." He went to the window and switched on the air conditioner. The building was one of your typical Midtown block-shaped, cookie-cutter apartments, each with an air conditioner and a fake fireplace and dining nooks that passed for cozy. For this, they charged nosebleed rents.

She was surprised that Kit put up with it. Up to now, he'd been the adventurous type who liked frequent changes of scenery. They had that in common, she thought. It was one reason she trusted getting semi-involved with him. She was starting to wonder about him, though. He was giving off the signals of a man who wanted to get serious and settle down.

"Remember, it's a sublet," Kit said when he saw her looking at the beige sofa, white walls and zebra-striped rug. Completing the picture were chrome lamps and an oversize framed cartoon graphic of a damsel in distress shooing Clark Kent away. The word balloon said I'm holding out for a hero.

I'm holding out for a chocolate bar, Sabrina thought. *Three hundred calories and six bites is all the commitment I can stomach.*

"How long are you planning to stay here?" she asked, wondering why she continually had to reinforce her flighty nature with him—and herself. It wasn't something she had to think about with other guys; it just *was*.

"Not long. But you know the Manhattan real estate market. I have a broker who keeps calling me up, trying to sell me on co-ops in the West Eighties just like this one. If I wanted that, I wouldn't be so eager to move. The kitchen's great, though."

Sabrina dropped her fringed suede bag on an armchair and parked her hands on her hips. She was out of sorts, spoiling for a fight, and she didn't know why. Her skin felt swollen and vaguely itchy. "You figure Decadence for a permanent job, then?"

"Nothing's permanent."

"So true." She hitched a shoulder. "What about the

chocolate shop you mentioned?'' An image flashed before her eyes: her behind the counter, plump and pregnant in an apron, an array of sweets displayed on pretty paper doilies. Crazy. Was her period due? She had to be hormonal to be getting ideas like that.

"The chocolatier's for my golden years, when I'm sick of working in restaurants.''

"Uh-huh. Whew.'' She wiped her brow. "I was starting to think that you're looking for a permanent situation.''

"Would that be so wrong?''

She blinked. "Not necessarily. For some people.''

"What kind of people?''

She motioned at the living room. "That kind.''

"There are other choices—it doesn't have to be one extreme or the other.''

"I'm all about extremes.''

His eyes ignited her as they traveled from her head to toe and back again. Her upper lip started to sweat. When she crossed her legs, her slippery thighs slid against each other, making her think of sex—wet and hot and wild. So, it wasn't PMS or chocolate overload or heat rash. It was Kit—under her skin like a thousand burning needles, tattooing every inch of her with his name.

"All or nothing?'' he said.

"More like all, then nothing.''

"Why is that, Sabrina? Why would you purposely set out to end up with nothing?'' His tone wasn't accusatory, only baffled.

"Not on purpose,'' she said. "That's just the way things end up.''

"I see." The concern on his face was enough to make her wish she could be different for him.

"I travel light," she stressed, even though she'd always believed that explaining yourself was a waste of time. "Making promises you can't keep will drag a person down every time." She blinked at him. "Hell, you should know. You're the same as me."

"I *was*," he said.

Briefly she closed her eyes, deciding in that instant to ignore his admission because it hinted at an area she didn't want to explore. She wasn't ready to think about Kit needing more than she could give. Even if, by some miracle, she actually won the bet with Mackenzie, staying in one place for an entire year wasn't enough to nullify the habits of her entire adult life. Adult life? She'd been like this since she was thirteen.

And what does that tell you?

Time to change your life, trust in faith, open your heart.

The cynic inside her gagged on the platitudes. *Oh, come on!*

Certain that it was time to change the subject, Sabrina purposely brightened her voice. "Hey, where's the chocolate? Wasn't I lured here to be..." *Seduced, if there was a God in heaven or a Gaia down here seeing to her more earthly pleasures.* "To be plied with a taste bud extravaganza?"

"I've got plenty of chocolate, if you're up for it."

There wasn't enough chocolate in the world.

"Bring it on," she said.

Kit nodded to the couch. "Make yourself comfortable."

"Can't I come into the kitchen with you?" Familiar territory. Not that she'd ever relied on safety, of course.

It was just that Kit scared her more than anyone or any thing she'd ever confronted.

Why? Because he made her want to surrender.

"No," he said, "I want this to be special. You deserve the full presentation."

He disappeared into a kitchen that was emitting the sweet smells of home-baked treats. She wandered into the living room. A low coffee table between the couch and the fireplace was draped in a silky cloth the color of peacock feathers. A dozen small ceramic dessert dishes were stacked on it, along with napkins, silverware, candles—unlit—and several bottles in an ice bucket.

Oh, boy. Kit was going through with it. Seduction by chocolate.

All she had to do was surrender....

The lights dimmed. She spun around. He was in the doorway holding a tray filled with desserts. "Don't look," he said. "Turn around, sit on the couch. Relax."

She sank onto the plush couch, listening for his movements. He placed the tray on the dining table behind her, then came around and lit the candles, on the mantel, on the table. She opened her mouth to question the evocative setting, then thought better of it. Why protest? Wasn't this what she wanted? Even with the regret of giving up the ring lingering at the back of her mind, the truth was that losing a bet couldn't get more rewarding than this.

"Lean back," Kit said, adjusting pillows.

Her shoulders remained rigid. He reached across the couch from behind and eased her deeper into the cushions, giving her a brief massage. Her head lolled, touching her cheek to the back of his hand.

"What's this about?" she whispered.

"Presentation."

"The luncheon guests will be in a ballroom dressed to kill, wearing shoes that pinch their toes. They won't be comfortable. They'll be bored."

"Then we'll give them a reason to smile."

Kit lifted her hair and dropped a quick kiss on her nape. A shiver spilled across her skin. Next something smooth and slippery caressed her neck. She reached up to feel for it just as he slid the scarf into place, covering her eyes. She inhaled sharply. A dark excitement took hold, deep inside her belly.

"A blindfold?" she squeaked. "What's that for?"

"To narrow your perceptions." His voice was low and velvety, soothing but also arousing. "I want you to concentrate on taste and scent." He knotted the scarf at the back of her head.

She lifted an edge, turning to peer at him as he retrieved the tray. His intentions might be more serious than she'd hoped for, but the man certainly had a fine butt—firm and muscled even in those loose cotton pants that were the next best thing to being naked. It was the kind of butt that made a woman forget her objections.

Kit held the tray too high for her to see its contents. "No peeking."

Piquing is better, she thought, wetting her lips as her interest in the proceedings spiked even higher. Mackenzie had practically given her the go-ahead. And ever since the afternoon with her parents, Sabrina was no longer so sure that their remarriage was a mistake in the first place. She'd been wrong about them, wrong about a lot of her mixed-up doubts. So why not let go and enjoy herself?

Flimsy justification, sneered her inner voice. *Where's your willpower?*

Maybe Kit would feed her lots of chocolate and she'd get it back. The ring was still at stake, after all.

"Let's start with something light," he said, settling on the cushions beside her. She was too aware of his proximity, drawn to him at the same time she recognized the need to maintain a distance if she didn't want this to go too far. The blindfold wasn't helping. It made her vulnerable, yet her senses were already so sharpened that the brush of Kit's arm across her knees felt like an intentionally sensuous caress.

Vague shadowy shapes showed through the lightweight scarf. There was a sliver of vision at the bottom edge. When she tilted her head back, she saw a blurred Kit, dishing up a small serving of one of the desserts onto a plate. She closed her eyes, consciously letting go of the tension that their earlier conversation had provoked. This wasn't about promises or commitments. It was about sensation. The pleasure of the moment.

Kit leaned closer. Her nerve endings zapped to full attention. "Open up."

She hesitated. Silly. It was only her mouth.

He slipped a bite of dessert between her lips. Cool, smooth and sweet, with a lemony tang. "It's good," she said as the airy confection slid down her throat.

"Another bite?"

She took it. "Yum. What is this?"

"Meringue with lemon curd. Almost no calories. We can pipe it into pastry puffs or make floating islands. The ladies will love it."

"I agree. Approval granted."

"Here's another." He nudged her lips with a fork.

She put her hands on his forearm, steadying herself, and obediently opened her mouth. "Mmm." Another burst of citrus flavor. "Lime?" she said. "I like it, but where's the chocolate?"

He withdrew. "Don't rush me."

She heard clinking as he switched plates. "Try this one."

Crisp crust flaked on her tongue, followed by a too-sweet bite of fruit. She swallowed. "Not my favorite."

"Peach tart," he said. "I can make them with straw-berries or kiwi—"

"No. There's nothing new about fruit tarts." Sabrina pushed up the blindfold with one finger and peered out at him. "Dominique wants Decadence to make a splash at this event."

Kit tugged the scarf lower, urged her hands back to her lap. "Don't worry. I've only just begun."

She swallowed grittily. "Give me the hard stuff."

"I guarantee you'll like this one." He leaned even closer, pressing against her as the familiar scent of chocolate reached her nose. Tongue extended, she made a reaching motion with her head, taking the op-portunity to arch her back so her breasts came into full contact against his chest. Two could play this game.

"Smells delicious, but I can't find it." Her voice was husky, teasing. She flicked her tongue in the air. "Put it in. I'm ready."

The sound that came from Kit's throat wasn't com-pliant, but he fed her without further comment. A dense, smooth and very cold cake melted on her tongue as an explosion of intense chocolate and coffee flavors contrasted with the sweetened whipping cream that topped it. Bittersweet chocolate shavings dusted her teeth and lips. She licked them, swallowing. "Mmm, that one's powerful."

"Chocolate fondant cake," he said. "I thought we could make them in bite-size molds, serve them up with a variety of other desserts so the guests can sample our entire offering without feeling greedy."

"Except that one bite isn't always enough, especially when the taste is that—" she shimmied against him "—decadent."

He was so close she could sense the movement of his lips, a whispered promise on her moist skin. "Are you greedy?"

"No, but I am selfish."

"What's the difference?"

"Greedy grabs. Selfish...savors."

He nudged against her thigh. "Savors all to herself, hmm?"

She moved her leg into the pressure, rocking her hips. Her hands found the hem of his jersey and she gripped it, holding on and slumping into the cushions as he leaned over her, inserting a thigh between hers, breathing against her neck as his hands ran across her shorts to the jumping muscles in her abdomen. He put his palm on her stomach, gentling her. His lips nipped at her collarbone.

"I want to savor *you*," she said, sighing, "mmm, all to myself."

"I've been here for the taking."

"Yes, but..."

He licked her lips until they opened, which, granted, didn't take long. Bet be damned. She was ready to sample every inch of Kit in bite-size gulps and long, luxurious licks. Delaying had only made her appetite more ravenous.

Instead of his tongue, he inserted another bite of the cake between her lips. "Your chin is covered with chocolate dust," he said, swiping it with his thumb. She heard a smacking sound. "Umm. You taste good."

"A kiss would taste even better," she purred. Part of her wanted to rip off the blindfold, but the lack of sight was heightening her anticipation. She couldn't be sure what he was going to do next—feed her or ravish her.

She twined her legs around his hips as he leaned away from her, obviously dishing up another serving. "Tilt your head back," he coaxed, and a stream of cool, sparkling water poured into her mouth. She sputtered in surprise and some of the water spilled across her front, but then she latched onto the bottle and drank lustily, feeling wonderfully catered to.

Kit withdrew the bottle. "That was to cleanse the palate." With a paper napkin, he blotted the water that had dribbled from her chin to her chest. The cleanup went on a little too long, possibly because her nipples were drawn into tight peaks that had to show beneath her ribbed white muscle shirt. Hmm, yes, his fingertips had grazed across her breast on purpose. With a last swipe of the napkin, he brushed one of the straps off her shoulder. Lashes tickling the scarf, she lowered her lids to peer down at her own chest. One side of the damp T-shirt was barely staying up, caught on the bump of her aroused nipple.

She smiled, wondering if she wasn't supposed to know that she was almost exposed, and pushed a bent arm beneath her breasts, making them plumper.

Kit's voice came near again. It was hoarse. "Having fun?"

"After this, I might have to get a job as assistant pastry chef." She squeezed him with one thigh; the other leg was tangled between his in a position that was casually intimate. As if they were already lovers.

"And I might have to hire you." He caught her chin between his thumb and forefinger, opening her mouth. "Here's a change in texture. Tell me what you think of this."

She chewed a combination of crisp cookie, icy sorbet and a garnish of very sweet orange. "Orange and almond?" she guessed. "It's scrumptious."

"You have good taste buds. This one's fluted almond cups, filled with blood orange sorbet, but we could serve mousse, zabaglione, fresh berries..."

"I can't decide—they all sound good." Her taste buds wanted to get back to the kissing.

He touched a fingers to her lips. She started to lick at it, but he tapped her and said, "We're still not finished." Again, he reached to the table, but quickly resumed the contact as he leaned over her to stuff a large bite of pastry into her mouth.

"Mmph." Although distracted by the erotic pressure between her thighs, she managed to absorb the melting mouthful of airy layers of cream and crust. A little chocolate, sweet vanilla...

"The traditional Napoleon—an old favorite of Ma'am's."

"Very French. The luncheon guests will love them, I'm sure."

He chuckled. "You're approving almost everything. And I *know* you know how to say no."

She smiled, reaching out to caress his arm. "It must be the blindfold. I have no defenses." She splayed her hand on his chest. He was warm, solid, giving. An impressive man in every way.

"Can I take it off now?" The candlelight formed a flickering glow behind Kit's dark shape as she bent forward, sliding her arms around his shoulders. With her mouth, she found his neck, his jaw, his ear. He tasted like vanilla and musk, of sweet and salty male.

He turned his head to catch her mouth. "Not yet."

At last, they kissed. A long, slow, deep—oh, so very deep—kiss. Although there was no hallelujah chorus or blinding instant of understanding, suddenly her tangled emotions didn't seem like such a barrier. Nor did the silly bet that really didn't mean anything at all. Pleasure swelled inside her, pure and uncomplicated. *This is what I want,* she thought, touching her fingertips to Kit's face as they kissed. She memorized him with her lips and her touch and her yearning heart. She didn't want a ring. *Just this man.*

Kit had scooped his hands under her derriere and pulled her all the way into his lap. He cocked his head back, laughing a little for no reason at all. She joined him out of sheer joyousness, peppering their laughter with small openmouthed kisses.

"Why are you laughing?" he asked, rubbing his palm in circles across her back. She worked her shoulder blades, preening under the attention.

"I don't know." Her lips moved over his stubbled cheek. Each prickle touched off a spark of delight inside her. "Because I'm happy?"

"Then my presentation went well?"

"It did." She tried to squint through the light blindfold, wanting to see his expression. "But the chocolate side of the menu was sadly lacking."

"Ah." He stretched an arm out to the coffee table. "Taste this, then. It's a homemade truffle."

She bit into the rich, velvety chocolate. Even though she'd learned to appreciate the wonders of chocolate the past few weeks, none had tasted as delicious as this. She rolled it on her tongue, savoring the intense flavor. Her lips smacked. "God, that's good. You made that from scratch?"

"Ma'am taught me. And her French grandfather taught her. He was a chocolatier in Lyon."

"Another, please."

"If you insist." He reached again, but instead of feeding it to her directly, he brought his lips to hers with the truffle between them. It bumped against her mouth before she opened to consume it, chocolate blending with their kiss in a fusion of the senses. They were loud and sloppy and greedy, eating at each other's mouth, trying to get deeper, go further. Not possible...with their clothes on.

Sabrina shoved the blindfold up past her eyebrows. Kit's face was right there in front of hers—eyes bright, mouth reddened and smudged with chocolate.

"I don't know how much more of this I can take." Her constant craving for him was an empty ache inside. She wanted him so hard it hurt. "Are we finished yet?"

His smile was wicked with seduction as he lifted another of the hand-dipped chocolates toward her mouth. "Ah, *chérie*. We've only just begun."

She pushed against his shoulders with all her strength, flattening him to the couch. Kit let out a "huh!" of surprise. The truffle went flying. She was already astride him and he wasn't putting up much resistance after the initial shock, so she felt safe reaching over to the table, her left hand pressed to the center of his chest to keep him in place.

Her other hand was shaking. She scanned the crazy quilt of half-eaten desserts, then seized on the perfect item, slipping her fingers around the handle of a small silver pot. It was warm.

"Look what I found." She held it up so Kit could see, tilting it a little so the chocolate sauce almost spilled from the spout.

"What are you going to do with that?" His eyes glittered in the candlelight.

"Take off your shirt and find out," she said, already sliding the football jersey up the clenched muscles of his midriff. *Oh, yum.*

9

IT HAD ALWAYS been Kit's philosophy to comply when a woman said, "Take off your shirt," and as exceptional as Sabrina was, she was no exception. He lifted his shoulders off the couch, skinned the Browns jersey over his head, wadded it up and threw it across the room.

"Nice," she cooed. Her fingertips danced across his stomach muscles as if she were playing a piano. The chocolate pot tilted at a careless angle and he tightened up, expecting the gooey splash any moment.

Her head ducked toward his midsection. He sucked in a half-frozen breath, finding the action so suggestive he instantly imagined her lips wrapped around him, sucking hard. He'd been sporting a raging erection for the past ten minutes and having her squirm around on top of him couldn't be good for his staying power.

She dropped a kiss on his stomach and popped back up. He covered his eyes and groaned. "You're playing with fire, woman," he warned, peering at her from beneath his clasped hands.

"Playing with chocolate," she said, and tipped the pot two feet above his chest. A thin stream of the dark brown sauce poured out, splashing against his skin. He flinched, although the sensation was pleasant. Even tantalizing. Oh, man!

A warm puddle of chocolate syrup had collected between his pecs and was beginning to run down the center of his rib cage. "Umm, you're dripping." She swiped the leading edge of the drip with a finger, then leaned over him and offered the chocolate to him. He wanted more than her finger, but it would do for a start. He licked carefully.

Sabrina shook her head at his precision. "That's not how you do it." Still holding on to the pot, she leaned over him and gave a broad stroke of her flattened tongue up his abdomen, slurping the runnel of chocolate sauce. It smeared on her chin and around her lips, and she grinned seductively at him as if she knew what he was thinking.

He caught the back of her head in his hand and pulled her toward his mouth. She lost balance and fell onto him, slithering against the chocolate. "We're getting messy," she said between kisses. "There's warm chocolate running down my arm."

He gripped her bottom. "Put the chocolate aside. We don't need it."

"I do."

"You can feast on me," he said. His lungs hurt. His body was on fire. She was pliant, moving around on top of him, as sinuous as a cat.

She lifted her head, smiling behind her disheveled hair. "Sure, that's what *you* want. What about me?"

"You prefer chocolate?" he said in disbelief.

"Mackenzie assures me it's better than sex."

"Mackenzie is an idiot."

"I know." Sabrina laughed. "Maybe someday she'll meet the guy who can explain the difference."

Kit shifted. "Your sister's sweet, but right now—"

"You want—"

"This," he said, easing his hand down the back of her shorts. Her butt was bare. He slid his palm across her satin skin, squeezing and kneading her. His fingertips found the narrow strip of a thong and slipped beneath the elastic, tugging the sexy underwear tighter. She let out a gasp. Blinked rapidly. Squirmed. Moaned. He didn't let up. "Gotcha," he teased.

"Let go."

"Not until you say—"

"*Please.*"

He shook his head. "Say yes." *Say you can love me.*

"Say chocolate," she panted, bringing the small silver pot up near his face. "Or I'll pour it all over you."

He gave the thong another tug. "As long as you lick it off…"

She sucked air between her teeth, grimacing with pleasure. "Contrary to all app—appearances," she said tipsily, "I am not a chocolate fiend."

"Coulda fooled me."

"It was only to delay—" she rocked against his erection and for a few seconds his vision fogged "—*this* from happening."

"Why?"

"Mackenzie and I—we had a bet. I mentioned it, didn't I? Part of my thing was to stay out of fast-food relationships until I—" She stopped in the middle of the explanation, blinking at him with surprise on her face.

"You know that I don't do fast food," he said, watching her warily. "I like home cooking."

"Home cooking." She was doubtful.

He kissed her gently. "Try it."

"I'm afraid I might like it too much."

"Hey." He let go of her thong and brushed the hair out of her face. Her cheeks were pink; her eyes were confused. "You're Sabrina Bliss. You can never get too much."

She drew a deep breath and sat up. "That's right." Exhibiting a talent for contortion, she peeled away her chocolate-stained shirt, getting it tangled in her hair. "Take off your pants."

"What?" he said, staring at her perfect breasts.

The shirt was hanging off her right arm. "Mackenzie made me promise to go for the chocolate every time my cravings started up." Now Sabrina was trying to untie the drawstring on his pants one-handed. "So if I dip you in chocolate...well, that's two birds with one stone, isn't it?"

"Dip me in chocolate?" he echoed.

Her hand was reaching toward his groin. "We are experimenting with desserts, are we not? I'm going to call this one Chocolicious."

KIT STARED at the wavy red mist on the ceiling until his eyes rolled back in his head. Okay. First had come the dancing colors and now he was so dizzy he could barely keep his eyeballs in their sockets. If Sabrina didn't quit toying with him soon his brain was going to be the first organ to explode.

"Sabrina?" His clutched at the blankets they'd thrown aside when they'd moved their show into the bedroom. "What are you—holy damn!" Premature exclamation. She'd squeezed him where she shouldn't have—at least with such emphasis—and now he was seeing stars. If rocket ships were next, he was signing up for a lifetime ticket.

"Slow down," she purred. "Don't be so impatient." With due diligence, she applied more chocolate, stopping to admire her work of art before taking a firm hold at the base of his erection and licking up and down the length of it as if he were a frozen fudge bar.

Kit let out a lusty sigh. *Finally.*

He was sprawled on the bed, naked except for chocolate sauce. She was crouched over him, wearing nothing but a thong and a smug, chocolate-smudged grin.

As he watched, she opened her mouth to take all of him in. Her cheeks hollowed and the suction was so incredible he had to grab at the posts of the headboard before he bucked them both off the bed. She pulled back a little, her tongue swirling around the head of his penis, then bobbed over him, up and down, her lips glistening with chocolate. His entire body tensed, then gave in to the coursing, wild rush of erotic sensation as he climaxed. Too much, he thought with what was left of his brain. It really was too much.

But that was Sabrina.

And that was why he loved her.

"Whew." She'd flopped over his sprawled legs to reach the bottle of water she'd set on the floor beside the emptied pot of chocolate. He squinted, lazily considering the way the glow of the neon city outside lit the curve of her buttocks. His gaze wandered higher, finding the chili pepper tattoo on her shoulder. Her throat rippled as she swallowed half the bottle of water in one unending gulp, the same way she'd—

He twitched, growing warm at the thought. Well. Wow. It wasn't taking him long to recover.

Sabrina threw her hair back from her face, glancing

first at his lower half and then up at his eyes with a grin. "Are you sure you're not eighteen?"

He plumped a pillow. "What can I say? You make me feel so young. C'mere."

She drank the remainder of the water first, then tossed the empty bottle and crawled up beside him. "What's on your mind?"

"Absolutely nothing. A hurricane went through and blew my brain clean. I can't even move."

"Hmm." She snuggled into him, lifting his heavy arm and putting it around her shoulders.

"Don't be so smug." He brushed his fingers over her breast. Maybe he *could* move. "Or I'll tell you what I'm thinking and that will really wipe the smile off your face."

"Ooh, threatening."

"A promise," he said, tweaking her nipple.

She turned onto her belly and looked closely into his eyes, possibly seeing something there that he couldn't restrain. "Kit. Don't go serious on me."

He tried to be as flippant as she. "Can I go seriously down on you?"

Her face pressed into his chest, muffling her voice. "I know what you want to say, but you can't. Every time a guy says it to me—" He felt her breath shudder against his skin. "I run."

"And this time you want to stay."

She clutched him, pushed one leg between his and moved sensuously, stroking him with her thighs. Hot, but he got the idea that seduction was the easiest way for her to relate. Except then she whispered, "I want to stay."

"Because you lost the bet?"

She looked up. "Technically, I haven't..."

He huffed. "We're not finished. Trust me, woman, this time you're going to lose the damn bet. You're not getting out of this bed until we're lovers—technically, and in every other way possible."

"I hope that's a promise." She wrinkled her nose, but the soft look in her eyes was a concession, whether or not she knew it. They would be lovers, and they would be in love. He'd see to both. Somehow.

She'd angled her head and begun kissing a path along his biceps to his shoulder, nuzzling his neck, her mouth getting hotter, bolder. "It's not the bet," she said into his ear. "It's you." Her tongue flicked his lobe. "I want you. I want—"

He put his hands on her hips and pulled her on top of him. Her honey-colored hair dragged across his chest like silk.

She brushed it aside again, showing him her face. "I want to stay with you."

"For as long as you like." He brushed a knuckle over her cheek. "Forever would be nice."

Sabrina heart clutched. "I warned you not to start talking like that. It's too dangerous." She'd run—she knew it. Even if she didn't really want to, she'd run. Three months she'd gone with her last guy, the longest ever, but as soon as he started talking about love and, even worse, hinting at marriage, she couldn't get out of town fast enough.

Disappointment crossed Kit's face, but thank heaven he didn't dwell on it. He leaned back on the pillow, shooting that sexy grin at her. "There's one way to shut me up."

"Tell me."

"First, you could get naked."

She reached down, peeled off the thong and dangled it in front of his face.

"That was quick," he said.

She whipped it over her shoulder. "What else?"

"Reach into that drawer over there—"

"I have to do all the work," she complained cheerfully, finding a box of condoms. Unopened. Interesting. How long had he lived in New York? Five months. This didn't bode well for the idea she was clinging to—that they were having fun sex, not making undying promises. Thoughtfully, she removed one of the condoms. Maybe he bought *lots* of new boxes. Which didn't sit well with her, either, come to think of it.

"Only because I like to watch you move naked," Kit said. His palm slapped down on her rear end as she swiveled around, sitting on her heels and tearing open the packet with her teeth. "Careful, tiger."

She removed the condom and threw the empty packet to the floor. The bedroom was going to be as big a wreck as the living room by the time they were finished. "And now?"

"I'm ready. Go on to the next step."

She looked down. Yes, indeed, he was ready. From spent exhaustion to full arousal in a matter of minutes and he hadn't raised a finger. The man was a race car...but now she was taking control of the stick.

She applied the condom, saying, "This isn't very romantic," to tease him.

He vaulted up from his prone position. "You want romance?"

"No, I—"

He kissed her, stopping the lie as soon as his tongue

touched hers. A great wave of relief rose up inside her. She wanted romance and she wanted love and she wanted hot, crazy sex, but most of all she wanted *him*, in her life forever with his cocky grin and his big, lonely heart and all those luscious muscles—muscles that bunched and moved beneath her hands as he pressed her down onto the bed. His mouth was still on hers, kissing romance into her soul the same way he stirred vanilla into chocolate.

"Whew," she said. "Whew. What was that?"

"As if you don't know," he muttered against her skin as he licked a spiral around her breast, teasing her nipple with flickering strokes until finally his mouth opened and she arched like a bow, all of her drawn into the heat and careening pleasure. It glowed in her veins. She must be lit up like a firefly.

"Give me more." She lay limp and spreadeagled, all energy lost in the fire that had melted her down to nothing but a need for pure sensation. Kit was it—his skilled hands touching her everywhere at once, his mouth sucking and licking and teasing shiver after shiver out of her, his body pushing hard into hers, molding her thighs around his so they were joined even before he'd entered her. She heard herself moaning. "More...more..."

There was no shock when he gave her what she asked for, only deep satisfaction as he slowly eased inside her, taking his time, doing it right. She felt as if her entire body had opened to him, and the exposure was both alarming and illuminating. She was unguarded, she'd let him in, but it was okay, for now, at least. It was okay because it was Kit's face looking down at her, his eyes reaching into hers, speaking, giving, loving, all without fear. Together, they were consummate, flawless, *whole.*

He thrust inside her, setting off sparks, building the fire. Soon it was a roaring blaze, and they were at the center of it, moving against each other and then with each other, tangling their gasps and probing tongues, their broken cries and deep caresses, until everything she was feeling had wound into a tight, clenching knot. Kit wrapped his hands around her hips and held her in a vise-like grip and drove deeper, touching her so perfectly her body rose even higher into the ecstasy of him and her, both of them together, and exploded in hot, shivering spasms that went on and on until she was drained.

Kit stayed on top of her, inside her. Delicious. She lay drugged, collecting her shattered perceptions, idly stroking his shoulder.

He kissed her forehead. ''Was that romance?''

''Sort of...''

''Was it love?''

With any other man, she would have said no, it was sex, but with any other man it *would* have been sex—far less miraculous sex—and for the first time she couldn't make herself brush off her feelings. It was easier before, when she was alone and separate, but now she was stuck—literally—and she cared as much about Kit as she did for protecting herself.

''It was love,'' she admitted.

''You don't sound happy about that.''

She pried herself away from him, the remains of chocolate having dried into glue. ''This wasn't what I'd planned.''

He shrugged. ''Me, neither.''

Her heart twinged. "Oh, really?"

"I wanted you from the first time I saw you, but I wasn't going to fall in love with you." He folded his arms across his chest. That bothered her; she wanted them around *her*. "No way."

"How come?"

"Isn't it obvious? You're a sorceress. You collect men's hearts as a hobby, and you don't even bother to keep them."

She shook her head. "They don't give me their hearts."

"Some of them do."

"How would you know? Men are—" She waved a hand in the air. "They're not in touch with their feelings, to coin a phrase. And neither am I. That's what bugs guys about me—I'm just like them."

"Then you're lying to yourself, just like some men do."

"About what?"

"Having no feelings."

She grabbed a pillow to have something to hug. "Maybe so. But then what about you?"

"I've been the same way, in the past—that's how I know."

She raised her eyebrows. "But you're not anymore?"

"I made a decision to change after Ma'am died. When I came to New York, it was with the idea that I was going to find a good woman and settle down, let myself have all the things I'd always wanted but didn't quite dare to try for. I don't know if it would have worked, but I intended to give it a shot, with the right woman."

Sabrina sat up, clutching the pillow in her lap. "Wait

a minute. Where do I come into this? You said this *wasn't* what you planned."

"You were going to be a brief affair. To get you out of my blood, that's all."

"That's all," she repeated. Familiar words. *That's all. No more. Only this. No, and no, and no.*

Speak them or hear them, it was one and the same.

She swallowed the lump in her throat, but all that did was move it to the pit of her stomach. She'd stopped wanting what she couldn't have—didn't dare try for, as Kit had put it—so many years ago that she'd come to believe she'd never wanted any of it in the first place. But that was all her relationship with Kit had been about—wanting.

Craving.

Needing.

Now their desires were fulfilled, which would have been enough for her once, but she wasn't so deluded that she'd fool herself into thinking she wouldn't want him again tomorrow. And maybe even forever.

Oh damn.

She drew in a shaky breath and looked at Kit, wary but so stuck she had no hope of making a clean get-away even if she wanted to try. "So...I'm not the 'good woman' you'd hoped for, but I am—what? A fortunate mistake?"

He caught her hand, pulled her onto his chest. His fingers smoothed over her hair as he studied her face, his expression both exasperated and awed. Her emotions lurched, so close to the surface she felt every upset and agitation as she never had before.

"Not a mistake," he said. "But you are so much more than I expected."

"I've always been less. I like being less." She lowered her head to rub her cheek against the hair matting his chest. The whirlpool in her gut was settling down. "I don't want to be a good woman. That sounds awfully dull."

Kit laughed. "Oh, shut up about that."

"Will you take a bad, bad girl *if* she promises to reform?"

"Are you promising?"

"I don't know. Give me some time to think about it, okay?"

"Whatever you want," he said, looping his arms around her and hugging tight. He began to talk about what they should do tomorrow, next week, a month from now.

She let him ramble without answering, even when he talked about getting a place together.

That was worrying, but Sabrina gave in, relaxing with a sigh. This was what she wanted, right? Kit's arms around her? A moment of safety and peace? It was all about herself, right?

It had better be. Because when she thought of Kit offering his brave, battered, solitary heart, she was afraid that—reformed or not—she couldn't hold it for very long without breaking it.

"CONFESSION TIME," Sabrina said with her head between her ankles. She closed her eyes and concentrated on breathing, expanding her diaphragm.

"You don't have to tell me," Mackenzie said, obviously trying not to grunt as she reached for her own ankles. "I can see."

"Shh," said the woman next to them, who wore bells in her dreadlocks.

Sabrina thought of white space. Cool, calm, empty. Kit kept intruding—hot, electric, solidly immovable. He came toward her, his apron filled with truffles, his eyes brimming with sly intent. Sex and chocolate—the perfect combination. She was craving both now.

"You don't *have* to give up the ring," Mackenzie whispered.

"But you've won. And that was the prize."

Mackenzie snorted as she straightened, wrecking her attempt at composure. "*I* won? Don't think so. We were supposed to decide in a year."

"Quiet please," the yoga instructor said in a sing-song voice. "We will now return to our *savasana*, the corpse pose...and relax. Our minds are silent. We are attuned to the cosmic energies."

"What happens now?" Mackenzie asked under cover of the jingling dreadlocks.

Sabrina lay prone beside her sister, eyes closed. "Nothing, except I pay up." She'd have to let go of the romantic dreams they'd both wound around the ring when they used to try it on in secret. Not so hard, considering that she'd just about forgotten she'd ever had them until her mother had awarded her the ring. If *she* kept it, the ring would get lost or stolen anyway. Mackenzie would treasure it.

"Now we slowly bring our legs up," the instructor said. "Hands behind our knees. And rock. Gently, please. We are stretching our spines, not crunching them."

Mackenzie clutched her bent legs above her and rocked on her curved back. Little spikes of damp hair stood up all over her head, making her look like a por-cupine. "Hmm," she said.

Sabrina straightened her legs so her toes touched the mat behind her head. She glanced sideways. Macken-zie was still doubled onto herself, scowling at the bulge of her tummy. "What does 'hmm' mean?"

The instructor strolled by. "Ladies, are we remem-bering to breathe from our abdomens?"

"So that's why my navel is whistling." With a giggle, Mackenzie let go of her knees. She collapsed onto the mat, plucking at her floppy T-shirt.

Sabrina straightened out, exhaling by degrees. "You think I'm going to split."

"No-o-o." Mackenzie's slow answer and private smile were aggravating in the extreme. Sabrina re-membered how her sister used to sit on her twin bed in the room they were forced to share at their post-divorce house, blinking her big eyes and saying noth-ing while Sabrina bounced off the walls, in a tizzy over the boy she loved/hated, a flaming rumor spread by a so-called friend, or another fight with their mom.

"Then *what?*"

Dreadlocks glared at them. "Zip it. You're screwing with my cosmic energy."

"Sorry," Sabrina whispered. "But this is important."

"And we rise," the teacher said from the front of the classroom. "We will end with our sun salutation. First *asana.* Positions, please."

The plinky-plocky New Age music and the smell of stale sweat and incense suddenly got to Sabrina. She grabbed her towel. "I can't concentrate on yoga. Let's get out of here."

Mackenzie was right behind her. "Thought you'd never ask."

"*Namaste*," Dreadlocks said, using the Hindu blessing with an inappropriate sneer.

"Yeah, that was nasty all right," Mackenzie said as they pushed past the swinging door into the dressing room. "My body was not made to twist that way."

"You did fine for a first-timer."

Mackenzie took a bottle of water out of her gym bag. "Let's get down to the important stuff. Was he good?"

Sabrina didn't hesitate. "Better than chocolate."

"How much better?"

"If you stacked Toblerones as tall as the Swiss Alps, he'd be ten times that."

Water sputtered from Mackenzie's mouth. "Wow," she said, scrubbing her drool. "There's a scale I can understand. Not from actual experience, mind you, aside from the Toblerones, but—" She blinked. "Wow. Good for you."

"Then what was the 'hmm' for?"

"You dolt. That was because you actually believe you lost the bet."

"Didn't I?"

"Do you remember what I said, back when all of this started? We were standing on the balcony at the Fontaine, watching Mom and Dad dance...."

"Sure I remember. You said no men."

Mackenzie *tsk-tsk*ed. "You never learned to listen before charging off like a runaway train."

Sabrina stopped in the middle of stripping off the leotard she wore over a sports bra and old leggings. She let the drooping straps fall to her waist. "All I remember is the no men thing."

"I said no *sleeping* with men...until you truly fall in love."

"Oh."

The dressing room grew so quiet the only sounds were the drip of the moldy shower stalls and the music from the yoga class. Mackenzie knew her better than anyone. If even *she* thought that Sabrina was in love with Kit...

Mackenzie nodded. "You see what I'm saying?"

Sabrina wondered if it was a faux pas to hyperventilate at yoga class. "Yeah," she said between breaths so shallow they would get her busted down to beginner's level. "I see."

But did she believe?

10

"*THIS IS YOUR SISTER'S* little candy store?" Kit said, standing agog at the crowded entrance to Sweet Something. He and Sabrina were bumped aside as more people arrived. "No wonder you made me dress up."

Sabrina checked him out. Even wearing off-the-rack, he compared favorably to the men in Calvin Klein and rock-star leather. Kit's shirt was made of a soft, silky material that clung just enough to show off his trim midriff and nice chest, in a shade of pale blue that made his eyes look brilliant.

He hadn't remembered to get a haircut, so his hair was longer than ever. But he'd shaved. She'd checked that out, too, in the back of the cab on the way over. The lipstick she'd carefully applied was probably smeared—or eaten away—but kissing Kit was worth it. She was bubbling with endorphins and she hadn't eaten chocolate in three days.

"Mackenzie's always been successful in her dogged way," Sabrina said, raising her voice above the chattering crowd and bouncy music from the jukebox—"The Candyman" as sung by Sammy Davis, Jr. "But this! Incredible. This is a truly spectacular success."

Kit squeezed Sabrina's hand. "Do you see her? I want to offer my congratulations."

Sabrina went up on her toes. "I think she's at the center of that crowd...." She pointed to a throng near the door, where flashbulbs were going off. "But we can find her later. Let her enjoy being the center of attention. She deserves it."

Kit watched as a couple of famous faces passed by. "Mackenzie knows all these celebrities? Isn't that the guy from *Law & Order?*"

"You watch TV?"

Kit put his mouth near her ear. "When you're not around to play with."

Sabrina flushed. "I told you this was going to be a splashy event. Mackenzie hired a publicist with great celebrity connections. It seems penny candy is very retro chic. The boldface Page Six crowd are all over it. Even Dominique and Curt are coming."

A waiter stopped in front of them, dressed in white and one of the Sweet Something candy-striped aprons. He offered a tray stocked with drinks of an unusual sort. The martinis sported an upended lollipop. The cinnamon/peppermint schnapps combo came complete with a candy-cane swizzle stick.

"They're called candy cocktails," Sabrina explained, surveying Grape Crushes and Mango Margaritas with colored sugars on their rims. Kit looked dubious, but he took two drinks and handed one to Sabrina. "*Salut,*" she said, sticking the lollipop in her mouth. "All the drinks are candy-themed."

"Any Chocolatinis?"

She shook her head. "Mackenzie's not selling chocolate, only penny candy. We'll be having no orgasms tonight."

Kit's arm went around her waist. "Don't count on it."

The sexy timbre of his voice gave Sabrina a thrill, but

she tried to concentrate on the party. This was Mackenzie's night to shine. Just as she'd sometimes been annoyed by her sister's Goody Two-shoes A+ record,
Mackenzie had suffered with being the overlooked sister when Sabrina's antics had hogged all the attention.
Seeing Mackenzie now—daring to take control of her
life, looking *mah*-velous, her store a smashing success—was a treat.

The store was stunning, a contemporary paintbox
done up in Willie Wonka meets Barbarella style. Sabrina had seen it in the midst of construction, but not
completed. The walls were splashed with blinding
color. A section of the second floor had been opened up
so the space soared to a balcony, which was reached by
climbing a stainless-steel spiral staircase. A series of
towering Plexiglass tubes acted as columns, each filled
with a different jawbreaker flavor or other candy.
There was a candy counter, but it wasn't the old-
fashioned type. This one was made of clear bins to hold
the candy, silver surfaces and colored tubing that
twisted up and around and overhead like a cartoon sci-
ence experiment. There was also a retro bubbler jukebox and small round tables and chairs in bright pri-
mary colors.

Sabrina scanned the party guests. "My parents
should be around, somewhere."

Nicole had called the past night to say they'd be
coming, catching Sabrina and Kit engaging in sweaty
naked aerobics on her futon. Her mother's voice had
sounded on the answering machine: "Sabrina, why are
you never home? I hope you're not staying out till all
hours. I called to ask what you're wearing—no jeans,
please, dear. You should have come shopping with

Mackenzie and me. Her stylist is amazing, she's made your sister look like a million dollars. What that woman could do with you! Mackenzie said you're taking that fellow Kit to the grand opening. Is this getting serious? Do tell him to shave, won't you—" *Beep*.

The phone had immediately rung again. It was Charlie, laughing, with his wife protesting in the background. "Never mind all that, Breen. We'll see you and Kit tomorrow night. Come as you are."

Sabrina and Kit had looked down at their naked, sweaty bodies, burst out laughing and collapsed out of their pretzel configuration.

"Hey, you two." Charmaine from the restaurant stepped out of the crowd and pulled a green lollipop from her mouth. Her lips were stained green, but that was from lip gloss, not candy. "I can't get over this place. And the celebrities—they're practically wall to wall. I'm stalking Ivar Whitman." She waved the lollipop, nearly getting it in the hair of a girl who'd fluffed herself to match the toy poodle tucked in her tote. "Onward, Vijay!"

Vijay smiled shyly and let Charmaine tow him away.

"I guess I'm not number one anymore," Sabrina said, making a mental note to tell Vijay to invest in a three-piece suit.

Kit squinted an eye. "You knew about that?"

"Of course. I can always tell when a guy has a crush on me. Except you. *You* let your chocolate do the flirting."

"Subliminal seduction," he said, looking sanguine.

Sabrina sputtered, swallowing a mouthful of martini. "You did that on purpose? I wasn't even sure that you liked me!"

"I liked you. But, if you remember, I was leery about getting involved."

She leaned against his shoulder, their arms entwined. "'Cause I'm bad."

He kissed the top of her head, lingering. "Nope. 'Cause you're too good."

"What's this?" Dominique Para slipped through a six-inch opening between guests. She was dressed in a shiny silver micromini and holding a tall glass of pink froth that matched her hot pink stiletto heels. "Are my employees consorting after hours?"

Kit grinned, not letting go of Sabrina's hand. "Vijay and Charmaine went thataway."

Dominique's lips narrowed. "I don't approve of this."

Sabrina started to get nervous. She wanted to keep her position at Decadence, and that had nothing to do with the bet. She'd once lost a job she'd loved as a riding teacher at a Virginia stable because the owner was a lech and his wife had blamed Sabrina when her husband couldn't keep his hands to himself.

"I'm teasing! I'm teasing!" Dominique's disbelieving laugh trilled up the scale. "Sabrina—the look on your face. I've never seen you anxious before."

"I wasn't—" Sabrina shut up. She *was* anxious. When there was nothing to lose, nothing mattered. It was easy to be careless and free. What a delusional dimwit she'd been before Kit.

"If it wasn't for workplace love affairs, the kitchen staff would have nothing to gossip about. Isn't that right, Kit?"

"Yeah. Although I'm not sure I've ever seen you in the kitchen, Dominique."

She pouted her lacquered lips at him. "True, true. I don't like getting the smell of food on my clothing. But it's the same in the modeling world. Sex makes the world go round—having it or talking about it." She winked. "Let me guess. You two don't do a lot of talking?"

"Dominique, quit torturing the help," said a deep male voice.

With that, Curt Tyrone appeared, his bald head shining inches above the other guests. He snaked a long arm around Dominique and gnawed kisses into her cheek, making silly grunting noises. He was the only one Sabrina had ever seen who treated Dominique like a regular woman, as if her beauty wasn't awe-inspiring.

Dominique's lashes fluttered girlishly. "Chefs don't like to be called help, Curt, dear."

"I don't mind," Kit said. "Just don't ask me to wash dishes."

Sabrina stayed silent and watched them chat about Mackenzie's store, the presence of dueling gossip columnists, the dessert menu at Decadence. Most of her time with Kit had been spent alone. She'd never seen him interact with this kind of crowd, but it stood to reason he'd be comfortable. He'd traveled all over the world and had worked in very upscale restaurants at jet-set locations. He was so natural and easy to be with, she didn't think of him as sophisticated. She thought of him as a vagabond, like herself.

Bonnie Gluckman, Mackenzie's hired-gun publicist, appeared to snag Dominique and Curt for photographs. "You should go, too," Kit said. "You're Mackenzie's sister."

"But not famous," she said. "I don't mind. Let's check out the candy."

They wended their way to the kooky outerspace candy counter. More of the workers in the colorful striped aprons were manning it, scooping out complimentary goodie bags for the guests. "Sen-Sen, Sweet-Tarts, Blo-Pops," Sabrina said, tapping the glass. Convex portholes set in the pink-and-orange walls displayed backlit hard candies, making them glow like neon artwork. "What's your favorite?"

Kit scanned the selection. "I don't remember having a favorite."

"Oh, come on. You must have."

"Jolly Ranchers," he said suddenly, spotting a familiar wrapper. "My mother used to keep them in her purse."

Sabrina asked a worker for a scoop of Jolly Ranchers and a handful of Pixy Sticks and Atomic FireBalls. She slipped a candy into her mouth and handed the colored cellophane bag to Kit. "To childhood memories."

He didn't take any. "Do you think we can escape this crush for a while?"

"Sure. We haven't explored the upstairs."

They ascended the spiral staircase. A number of guests had also come up, but they clustered near the tubular steel balcony railing, where the tables were. Sabrina took Kit's hand and led him to Mackenzie's office. It was neat and spare, painted white with soft gray carpeting. The furnishings were traditional—none of the wacky color explosion of the public areas.

"This looks more like Mackenzie," said Kit.

"Oh, she might surprise you. I think there's a wild child inside her crying to get out. How else could she think up Sweet Something?"

"A circus nightmare?"

Sabrina laughed. She sat on the edge of the desk, crossing her legs silkily. There were louvers in the door, so they could still hear the jukebox. A slumberous, velvety voice was singing about how much he liked sex and candy. The steamy lyrics were making her veins thrum with wicked ideas.

"Where's the candy?" she asked. "I'll have another piece, please."

The cellophane crinkled as Kit walked toward her, reaching inside the bag. He unwrapped a green apple Jolly Rancher. "Giving up chocolate?"

"I've lost my craving." She opened her mouth and he dropped the candy inside, then followed with his mouth, kissing her with a languid ease that matched the throbbing music.

The combination of sweet and heat made Sabrina's head swirl. She held on to Kit's belt, letting the kiss lift her, spin her, swallow her. The piece of candy slid against their tongues, melting as they sucked and licked at each other, humming with pleasure.

Kit stopped long enough to say, "Nothing against Mackenzie, but how long do we have to stay?"

"You're not enjoying the party?"

"I'm enjoying you more." He cupped her face. She nipped at his thumb. "I'm not into this glamour stuff."

She hooked a leg around the back of his knees. "What are you into?"

He groaned. "That's a loaded question."

"Seriously." She plucked at his shirt, loosening it

enough so she could slide a hand past the buttons and play xylophone on the ridges of his abs. "Between the Navy and your career, you've been around the world...."

"And I found out that home is the best place to be."

"Home?" She thought of her parents, trying to re-create the home they'd thrown away.

"I know I don't have a home yet, but I can make one. All I need is a wife."

Oh, she'd walked straight into that one. The thing was, she was attracted as much as repelled. Maybe more. Definitely more. "Just any old wife?"

"I have one in mind."

"How will you get her to stay?" She kept her voice light, but he must know there was a purpose to the question.

"I'll put her in a pumpkin shell."

"And there he kept her very well?"

"It could happen. She might even like it."

Don't bet on it.

"Let's have another piece of candy," she said. "I think I swallowed the last one when you put your tongue down my throat."

"No, I swallowed it when you licked my tonsils."

"Mmm. Yummy." They laughed, hugging on top of the desk.

"Maybe we should go and find Mackenzie and your parents," Kit said after another kiss. "Before our disappearance becomes too obvious."

"And I thought we were going to have desktop sex."

"Not in your sister's office. But I'll buy you a house with a desk, if you want. It'll be hard on my knees, but I won't complain. Anything for the little Mrs."

"You're cracked, Kit." Sabrina laughed brightly, to show what a joke she thought he'd made. She cast a longing look at the desk as they left the office. "Mackenzie wouldn't mind. Well, maybe she would, but she'd just whip out a bottle of disinfectant and spray until the sex cooties were annihilated."

Sabrina turned in time to see Mackenzie coming up the stairs, with Charlie and Nicole right behind her. Mackenzie's expression was strained, but Sabrina couldn't tell if that was opening-night jitters or if her sister had overheard the careless comment and was offended. Big mouth strikes again.

"Hi, you guys. We were just coming to find you." The group exchanged handshakes and hugs. Sabrina hugged Mackenzie. "So proud of you, Sis. The store is gorgeous. I never expected it to be so stylish and attract such attention."

"There are reporters here," Nicole said. Her face was flushed with excitement. "The party will be in the gossip columns!"

"That's just because of the celebrities, not me." Mackenzie seemed flustered by the attention.

"But the stars came out because of you, Kenzie." Charlie slung his arm around his youngest daughter's shoulders. "Sweet Something is a giant hit."

"Enjoy it," Sabrina whispered, squeezing Mackenzie once more.

"It's so overwhelming."

Nicole was hanging over the balcony railing. "Look—Rudy just opened a bag of Sugar Babies."

"She's so starstruck she's giddy," Charlie said, going to grab his wife before she toppled into the crowd below.

Sabrina laughed and linked arms with her sister as they also moved to the railing to overlook the glittering party. "I'm thrilled for you."

Mackenzie's eyes were huge. "It's a much bigger deal than I ever imagined. A reporter asked to come back next week to interview me and get photographs of the store. I feel like I'm dreaming."

Sabrina looked for Kit. He was talking to her parents nearby. "And to think this all started with our crazy pact to change our lives. Now you have this incredible store—"

"And you have Kit."

"Hmm."

"Hey." Mackenzie stuck out her chin. "What does that mean?"

Sabrina's voice lowered. "He's getting serious awfully fast. Already talking about buying a house and—and…" The hair on her nape prickled. She couldn't make herself say *marriage* out loud. "Usually this is when I start getting antsy."

"And are you?"

"A little."

Mackenzie considered. "Will chocolate help?"

"Ha! No way. I definitely don't need any more endorphins right now."

"But it will give you a nice little afterglow…."

"You have no idea, Mackenzie."

"Right—I'm too busy scrubbing up the sex cooties to bother with the aftereffects."

"Aw, hell, you heard that. I'm sorry, but c'mon, you know I was only kidding around. Don't be mad. I didn't mean to put a damper on your big night."

"I'm not mad. Not at all." Mackenzie smiled. But

she'd spoken in the same voice that Sabrina—and their mother—used when they didn't want to face what was right in front of them.

"I'm sorry, Kenzie. You'll find someone."

"I had Jason."

"You'll find someone who makes your heart beat double time."

"Girls, come here!" their mother called. "The photographer wants our picture."

"Sure." Sabrina turned to Mackenzie, fixing her hair and fussing with her dress—an understated sheath with spaghetti straps. Quite formfitting. It revealed a va-va-voom figure-eight shape that Mackenzie's previous baggy outfits had turned into an amorphous blob.

"Hurry," Nicole urged.

"Is Mom just a little too excited?" Sabrina said with a grin.

Mackenzie rolled her eyes. "It's the Manhattan hype. She's talking about working here. I told her that wouldn't be smart, with her diet and all, but..."

"Just remember you're in charge."

"I will," Mackenzie said. "I mean, *I am*."

They posed standing near the railing while the photographer snapped shots from down below. After a few photos, Sabrina remembered to look for Kit. She spotted him standing off to the side, leaning against the wall, looking like the lonely boy on the playground. In the past, she'd ripped up or burned every ex-boyfriend photo, but suddenly she knew she had to have a picture with Kit that would last forever, come what may.

"Hold on," she said. "Can we get a photo with Kit?"

She called him over. He shook his head, but came anyway. "I'm not part of your family."

"Not yet," Charlie said, trying for a fatherly menace that became a good-natured smile. "But you're going to make an honest woman of my girl, aren't you?"

"I'll do my best, sir."

"No paternalistic lectures, please." Sabrina took Kit's arm. "We're not even that serious."

"Yes, we are," Kit said, Mr. Implacable.

Sabrina gritted her teeth and smiled for the camera, hemmed in on both sides. Her father's arm was around her shoulders and Kit held her hand tightly. She couldn't beg off, she couldn't bolt. She couldn't even jump.

She was stuck, seduced by chocolate into falling in love.

"WHERE WERE YOU all afternoon?" Sabrina asked a week later, lying on her futon with Kit. The city was having a heat wave—record-breaking temperatures for the end of May. The window was open, the fan was on high, they'd just come back from an air-conditioned early movie, and she was still hot. Hot and restless. Since she was too dragged out to move, she had to talk.

Kit took his time answering. "You had that meeting with Daffy." Some answer.

"Daffy? With her assistant, is more like it."

His beer bottle clunked on the wood floor as he set it down. She didn't even have a table. What kind of adult was she?

"How'd that go?" Kit asked.

"They love your desserts. The assistant inquired

about you, wondering if you cater private parties. Daffy wants to have one where all they eat is dessert."

"Huh."

"*Very* posh."

"I could use the money."

Sabrina watched the whirring fan blades. Kit was being mysterious again. Over the past few days he'd continued dropping comments about making their thing serious, exchanging keys, moving in, having Sunday dinners with her family, and she'd kept silent. He went on, oblivious. She'd sensed the real need in him to become normal and settled, with the wife and kids and house in the suburbs. She'd even caught him reading the real estate section, and when she'd asked he'd been all excited about hardwood floors and working fireplaces.

Except now, he must have picked up on her nonresponsive hints.

Now *he* wasn't talking.

"What for?" she asked.

"My new place."

"Is that where you were? I saw the broker's name and office number on a pad by your phone."

He didn't answer, except for making a noncommittal sound.

She sighed. "I'm hot."

"It's cooler by the water."

Aha. A clue. "I know you do pretty well, but only millionaires can afford river views."

"Mmm."

Sabrina clamped her mouth shut. Okay, she wouldn't talk either.

A couple of minutes passed as they listened to the

sounds of screeching traffic, sirens, music from the open-air cantina down the street and a scuffle between street toughs. Tempers were rising faster than the mercury.

After ten minutes, she couldn't stand it anymore. "I know my place is too small."

Kit stretched his arms overhead. "Yeah. Look—I can touch the walls with my feet and my hands at the same time." The musky scent of his perspiration hung in the heavy air.

She breathed, liking it. "Congratulations."

"It's okay. You won't be here very long."

"You got that right." Even though Mackenzie continued to insist that Sabrina hadn't actually lost the bet since she was in love with Kit, Sabrina wasn't so sure. As soon as she relinquished title to the ring—and she would, any day now—she'd be free to move away whenever she wanted. Go somewhere cool and breezy, with palm trees and cabana boys.

Sabrina lay very still, careful not to brush her skin against Kit's. It seemed that every drop of sunshine absorbed by the brick building had poured into her tiny two hundred square feet. Even the brand-new sheets felt sweaty.

"I should go out on the balcony."

"You're naked," Kit said.

"That might give the neighbors a reason to stop yelling." She lifted a lazy hand, let it drop. "Maybe later."

He touched his fingertips to her thigh. "I could run you a cold bath."

"Ugh. The water's too brown."

He stroked her damp skin. She meant to tell him that she wasn't in the mood to fool around, but then it started to feel good. She gazed out the window, watching as the bricks turned from red to brown to black in the fading light. A glow rose from the streetlights below. Kit continued stroking, making concentric circles on her inner thigh without actually upping the ante. Her fingers curled into the wrinkled sheet. One long, continuous hot shiver was running up and down her body, making her scalp prickle and her soles tingle and every nerve ending in between scream with silent need.

She shut her eyes, trying not to shudder. "How long do I have to work before I get a vacation?"

"A year. Where do you want to go?"

"Somewhere wet."

"Me, too," Kit said in a hoarse voice. He touched between her legs.

She moaned, dissolving. "Would you come with me?"

"*Yes.*"

She spread her thighs, bringing one leg in contact with the hot skin of his abdomen. He sucked in a breath. His boxer shorts were tented.

"If I can't take it—" She panted. "The city, I mean. The job. If I have to go, if I leave—" Kit's fingers danced in her. The heat rose. She twisted on the futon, flinging her arms and legs carelessly in all directions.

"Stay with me," he pleaded, and she wasn't sure if he meant right then, or later. Always?

Her lips moved. Her voice rasped. "We could go away together."

"I want you here."

"Deeper," she said. She wanted him inside her. No matter what, always inside her.

He leaned over her. She pressed a burning kiss to his shoulder.

He breathed against her hair. "You feel as sleek as an otter."

"You taste like salt."

"You're slippery."

"Hold on anyway."

"I'm never letting go."

Sooner or later, we all do, she thought, but he was opening her, and she was breathing fire into her lungs and it was impossible to talk. He thrust inside her like a blade of white-hot steel and the sharp pleasure of it made a blinding arc through her body as she sobbed his name, coming in a rush until she was dizzy with pulsing heat and this senseless, idiotic, accidental love that simply refused to go away no matter how carelessly she disdained it.

11

"WHERE'S KIT?" Charmaine asked, rolling a large cart filled with trays of covered foil pans into the prep area they'd been assigned by the hotel. Sabrina checked Entrées—Turkey Breast with Green and Black Olives off the list. Her clipboard and headset were making her feel very efficient.

"I don't know," she said, trying to sound less irritable than she was about her pastry chef going missing. Two weeks had gone by, and she still didn't know what Kit was up to.

"He was in at 5:00 a.m. three mornings in a row doing advance work." Charmaine transferred the trays onto the counters. Everything had been prepared at the restaurant, since the hotel's facilities weren't top-notch according to Mario Alfieri. The entrées would be reheated just before serving. "Maybe he needed a break."

That was true. Knowing the International Relief Organization event was Sabrina's first big job, Kit had worked overtime. Still, she fretted. "He should have told me where he was going."

While Charmaine went to unload the desserts, Sabrina dialed the restaurant on the cell phone connected to her headset and spoke briefly to her stand-in. Kit wasn't there, but the lunch prep work was proceeding without incident.

Charmaine rolled the refilled cart into the room. "No word?"

Sabrina shook her head, gnawed by nerves. She'd always been a cheerful worker, but it was rare for a job to mean more to her than a way to pay the bills. All the talk of growing up and taking responsibility had gotten to her—she wanted to be a success, for once.

Charmaine was unloading. "This is the last of the desserts. I'll put the delicate ones into the fridge."

Sabrina slipped the cell phone back in her apron pocket and ran a finger down her list, checking desserts off as she went. "We're all accounted for—except the hand-dipped chocolates. Do you have them?"

On their day off, she and Kit had made the chocolates together, cooking fondant filling, spreading ganache on a marble slab. While showing her how to swirl the appropriate design on each bite-size piece, he'd told stories about cooking with Ma'am. Apparently he'd taken a wicked teasing from his outlaw friends when word had leaked out that he wore an apron and made Christmas chocolates. The taunts had included being signed up for a club called the Future Homemakers of America. Sabrina had laughed, but she'd also seen how much the memories meant to him. And what cooking represented.

"The chocolates are here," Charmaine said, lifting a large box from the top shelf of the cart. "But I don't have plates or bowls. In fact, I don't know how we're serving any of the desserts."

"That's Kit's department. He's planned something special."

"Then he'd better get here soon and fill us in."

"I know." Sabrina tapped her pen on the clipboard.

"This isn't like Kit. He also has to construct the center-piece for the main table. We've only got a couple of hours."

"Don't worry—I've served at a hundred of these events in my illustrious career as a wanna-be, never-was actress and it never seems like it'll get pulled together, but it always does." Charmaine flashed a cheery grin. "Aside from the time I dropped hot soup in the deputy mayor's lap."

Sabrina groaned as Parker, Vijay and a crew of servers arrived, crowding the catering kitchen. They said, no, there was no sign of Kit, so Sabrina allowed Charmaine to haul her out to the ballroom.

"Let's check tables and go over the menu with the staff," Charmaine said, with a gentle pat. "You need to stay occupied."

Fortunately, the room was lovely—and nearly finished. The florists had departed, leaving rustic yet elegant displays that featured exotic flowers and foliage springing up from circlets of twigs and berries. Crisp blue linens set off the sparkle of crystal stemware and shining white dinnerware.

Charmaine and Sabrina vetted the sea of round tables, making small adjustments as they went. The long rectangular table where the charity board members and award recipients would be seated was backed by a banner featuring the spiral and globe that was the IRO logo.

The only flaw in the setup was the big empty spot in the center of the table, where Kit's pièce de résistance was supposed to go. Sabrina stared at it in consternation, expecting Daffy DeMarche and her assistant to breeze in any minute and pitch a shrieking, goblet-shattering fuss.

Vijay poked his head through the doors. "Kit's here."

Sabrina clasped the clipboard to her chest. "Thank God."

Charmaine winked at her. "Never a doubt."

Sabrina passed her the clipboard. "You handle any last-minute questions. If Daffy shows up, tell her everything's perfect. I'm going to see what kept Kit and how far behind schedule he is."

"We've still got at least two hours before desserts are served."

"Yeah, but I need the centerpiece *now*," Sabrina said as she hurried off.

KIT WAS DUMPING six cups of sugar into a heavy saucepan when Sabrina flew into the room. "Kit, you're late! Where have you been? I need you—"

He wished.

"—to get the centerpiece dessert ready. Right now. You're not doing something with an ice sculpture, are you? Because I really can't handle the thought of it dripping all during the speeches—"

"Calm down. You sound like your mother."

She snapped her mouth shut.

The sugar was starting to melt. He checked the heat and began stirring.

"That was a low blow," Sabrina said. Her fiery expression didn't go with the sleek hair and sedate navy dress. He thought of how she'd ridden him last night like a warrior princess, her hair long and loose, blowing in the breeze from the fan he'd hauled up to her place. That was when he'd figured out what had been wrong the past weeks, when he'd thought she'd like an apartment by the river.

Sabrina tapped her foot. "Where were you?"

He wasn't ready to tell her yet. He'd have to show her.

"You took off without telling me—or anyone." Her forehead creased. "Now I know why my mom used to get so mad when Dad would disappear on one of his adventures. He *was* unreliable. I always thought she was being a harridan about it, but—" Sabrina stopped and made a face. "Damn. I do sound just like her. I always thought I was like my Dad, but I guess it's not so clear-cut."

Kit felt her eyes on him. She made a sound of frustration. "You're not saying anything."

"I can't talk now, I have to stir."

"You can stir and talk at the same time."

"I can listen," he said.

"No, I've said enough. We have a job to do. What are you making?"

"Caramelized sugar."

"Uh-huh. Daffy is expecting something grand."

"This will be." Kit stirred, checking the color of the melted sugar. At the precise moment, he took the pan off the heat and threw in a splash of hot water. "See the bowls?"

Sabrina looked at the industrial-size stainless-steel bowls he'd upended and coated with oil. "What are they for?"

"Watch." He chose a clean spoon and dipped it into the caramelized sugar, then drizzled the hot goo over the first bowl, going around and around until he'd created a fancy spider web design. He did the same with the second bowl, then moved on to the oiled plates and smaller bowls that Vijay had been setting out on the counter.

"I don't get it," Sabrina said.

"These will be the individual serving pieces for our desserts," he explained. "After the caramel hardens, we pry them off the molds. They'll be delicate and easy to shatter—that's why I had to do them here."

"I see." Sabrina still looked dubious. "How long does this take?"

"Ten, fifteen minutes." Working quickly, he and Vijay drizzled the caramel over the array of dishes, making random swirls and crosshatches.

"We need the centerpiece right away," Sabrina said.

He shot her a grin. "Don't be so impatient."

"Don't be so mysterious." She touched a fingertip to the glistening golden spider web he'd created around the upturned bowl. "Did your sudden disappearance have anything to do with the real estate broker who's been leaving messages on your machine *and* calling at the restaurant?"

"Not exactly."

"Are you ever going to tell me?"

"Maybe—if it matters to you."

"Obviously it does."

"Hmm…"

Sabrina screeched, "Man, I hate that!" and charged out of the kitchen.

"She's worried about the luncheon," Vijay said.

Kit grunted. "A little frustration will do her good."

Vijay scraped the bottom of the pan. "So…where did you go?"

"To the marina. But don't tell Sabrina—she thinks I'm buying a stuffy apartment and she's nervous as a cat."

SABRINA WATCHED from the back of the ballroom as the servers circulated with the miniature desserts, each one presented on a caramel candy plate. The larger, lacy bowls had been set out on all the tables, filled with an array of hand-dipped chocolates. Delighted guests had been snitching the flavored truffles while they waited for Daffy to wrap up the presentation.

Sabrina focused on the main table as Kit slipped into place behind Daffy. He'd really come through. The dessert centerpiece was a chocolate globe that had been made ahead of time and refrigerated. It was filled with chocolate mousse and decorated with edible hand-painted designs, which had been amazing enough on its own. But then Kit had set the basketball-size globe several feet above the table on a narrow pedestal and encased it within two halves of a caramelized-sugar shell. The effect was a tour de force takeoff of the IRO logo—the edible chocolate globe nestled within a spiraled cage that looked like golden filigree. The presentation was spectacular. The guests were most complimentary, and even Daffy had been satisfied.

Finally the woman concluded her closing remarks and stepped away from the podium to a round of applause. She took the knife Kit handed her, and with a flourish shattered the filigree of the globe. The guests cheered.

Kit took over from there, removing the globe to a waiting dish and slicing into it, serving portions topped by fragments of the shell. Sabrina went up to help.

Daffy leaned back in her chair, guiltily licking mousse off her lips. "We did it! Dominique's the best. And that chef of hers—ooh la la!"

"Kristoffer Rex," Sabrina said proudly, sending a smile over to Kit. He looked up, his eyes glinting in the way that made her heart turn over. "Remember his name."

SABRINA TWIRLED like a little girl on the cement walkway, her hair and long skirt floating free. "Hey, baby, you're a star!"

Kit strolled with his hands in his pockets. "And you're giddy."

"True, but I really mean it. You're going to be a famous chef." She capered. "You can write cookbooks, hobnob with the rich and famous, make lots of money, appear on *David Letterman*—no, I know! You can have your own cooking show." She sprinted ahead of him, turning, spreading her arms wide. "'Seduction by Chocolate with Chef Kristoffer Rex.'"

He laughed. "Will you endorse me?"

"You betcha!" She inhaled the sea air, then stretched up on her tiptoes, reaching for the dusky pink sky. "I'll verify it to the world. I am one well-satisfied customer."

"Ah, but you deserve your share of the credit. I talked to Dominique after the luncheon and she was very pleased with the job you did." Kit caught Sabrina's arm and pulled her to his side as they continued walking alongside the marina. He gave her a squeeze. "She said you handled Daffy like an old pro."

"My scattered work history finally came through for me." Sabrina was as buoyant as the ducks bobbing near the pier. "Who knew that handling a mistake-prone magician, a green-broke gelding and a tray full of triple-thick strawberry shakes would give me the skills necessary to please a finicky socialite?"

"Not to mention temperamental chefs and a staff of waiters who are all wanna-be actors or artists."

"Don't forget Dominique and Curt..."

"And me," Kit said.

"I had lots of help," Sabrina murmured, dropping her chin on his shoulder.

"Except with me."

She laughed. "Unless you count chocolate."

"Only when I'm wearing it," he teased.

"Mmm-mm, good. I do believe you look best in milk chocolate."

"But you haven't tried me in ganache yet."

She stepped back a little, sliding a nearly shy glance at him. Her throat was tight. "Well...I might be around to experiment with further recipes. Guess what?" She reminded herself to breathe, yoga-style. "Dominique asked me if I want to manage the dinner shift. Just on weekends at first. It would mean longer hours, but better experience and more money...."

Kit blinked, playing up his astonishment. "Job security? Just imagine. You could get a couch. And dishes."

He *would* think domestic! That was not where she wanted to go. "Ah, but I haven't said yes."

His voice dropped. "You still don't know if you want to stay?"

"It's just..." She searched for the words that would explain her need to feel free, as if she could take off at any moment. Even if she didn't actually *do* it, she wanted to be able to. The more connections and possessions she had, the more tangled up she got, the harder it would be to get away.

If she started wanting too much, and actually got what she wanted—

What? she thought. Did she expect devastation, disaster? Divorce? No one ever said life was fair. Or even safe.

She looked at Kit. But it could be beautiful.

"It's just that I need to feel free," she blurted. There. Not so difficult after all. She wanted love, and she wanted liberty. No problem at all combining the two. Right?

All Kit said was, "I know." He stopped and looped his arms around her waist. She expected him to kiss her, but instead he turned her toward the river. "We're here."

"The marina? What are we doing here?"

"Come on." He took her hand and led her onto the pier, producing a key that got them past a locked metal gate. They walked down the wooden ramp to the floating docks. The choppy water lapped against pilings and boat hulls. Tall masts with neatly furled sails loomed against the early-evening sky. Day sailors bustled about, swabbing decks and, she supposed, battening down hatches.

Kit was being mysterious again. She shaded her eyes with a hand and scanned the seaport. Rays of the setting sun rebounded off skyscrapers, splintering where they hit the water. "What with all the calls back and forth with the real estate broker, I was sure you were going to show me an apartment."

"You're half-right. I did meet a broker earlier today, when I was late getting to the hotel. But not a real estate broker."

"I saw her name and number on your notepad, remember?"

"Right. At first I thought we should buy an apartment in the city. I knew you were reluctant, but I had an image in my head of the perfect home—not too big, maybe even a little shabby, but with a warm kitchen with a gas range, an overstuffed sofa in the living room, a big pine four-poster featherbed, a nursery..."

Just stuff, she thought. *Consumer goods to weigh me down.* But she knew it wasn't the furnishings Kit wanted—it was the security of being a family.

He believed in that, as strongly as she did not.

"What changed your mind?" she whispered, pushing her hair back from her face. Why were they in a marina, if he wanted the solidity of a home?

"I started thinking about what *you* wanted instead."

Her heart dropped like a stone. "Oh, Kit, I never asked you to give up your dreams for me—"

"That's the beauty of this boat," he said. His eyes reflected the sunlight, refracting like the river. "It's the perfect compromise."

"What?" she said, her voice barely a whisper. "What?"

"This is our sailboat. Or it can be, if we decide to sign the purchase papers."

We. Sabrina stared at the boat moored in a nearby slip. Never, ever had she imagined this. The sailboat was a gleaming white, with polished brass fittings and teak rails. The name was painted at the bow: *Voyageur.*

"Care to board?" Kit took her hand and helped her

climb the walkway onto the deck of the boat. It rocked in the water, but she kept her balance easily, remembering long days at sea when she'd lived in Mexico and had become friends with various adventurers who'd made their boats their homes. She'd even crewed on a sloop that had sailed down the coast—one night in the dark, she'd told the tale to Kit like a bedtime story. Obviously he'd remembered it.

"I don't believe this." Her heart hammered when she saw the ice bucket and bottle of champagne waiting for them. Kit was serious. He would do anything to please her.

"The best of both worlds," he said, looking a little anxious, but valiant. "You get your freedom, I get my home. We can live aboard. Down below, there's everything we need—a galley, a small salon, even a cabin with full-sized bed. It's not large, I'll admit, but bigger than your apartment—"

"Everything's bigger than my apartment."

"And of course you can come up on deck and have all the space your heart desires."

"What about winter? Surely you can't live on a boat in New York in the winter."

"There are options. One would be to take jobs in a warm-weather climate. We could simply pull up anchor and sail away—any time we wanted to. We get tired of Florida, we sail to Mexico. I'd love to show you Tahiti. I can see you dancing on the black sand with frangipani in your hair. If you got bored, we could change coasts. Continents. We could go anywhere at all." He stepped closer and wound a hand through her hair, cradling her in his warm embrace. "You'd never have to feel tied down, I promise."

Sabrina looked up at him, awash with so much appreciation that her eyes welled. "Kit...I don't know what to say...."

"Say you love me."

"Oh, yes, I do. I love you. But I don't understand you. Abandon your job and your plans for the future? Live in impossibly cramped quarters? Always on the move? Why would you give up on your dreams just for me?"

His hand touched her hip, and she leaned against him with a sigh, nestled to his chest as the wind and water rocked the boat beneath them. Kit kissed the top of her head. "Because *you* are my dream, Sabrina. It's more important to me that we're together than all the rest of it combined. Besides, you're forgetting that I'm a Navy man. I spent a lot of time on the water in Tahiti—sailboarding and snorkeling. I even had a catamaran for a while."

"But what about Decadence, and your chocolate shop?"

"They won't disappear."

"What about—" She squeezed her eyes, her fingers clenching on his shirt. "Me?"

He angled his head to look into her face. "You?"

"What if I—if even this boat is too much and I—I—"

"Run out on me?" Kit supplied. He shrugged. "I'm betting you won't."

"I'm not a sure thing," she said with gravel in her throat.

"None of us are, but I'm willing to take the chance."

"Kit, are you asking me..."

"Yes, I am. I'm asking you to marry me. But if that panics you, I suppose we can try living together first.

Just be warned, I plan to feed you chocolate every day and make love to you every night until you're so addicted to me you couldn't imagine leaving.''

Right then, leaving was the last thing she wanted. But making a promise that must last forever...that was scary stuff. She couldn't make her mouth say the words.

Kit left her to uncork the champagne. He poured two glasses and held one out to her. "Should we check out the living quarters?"

"Not right now. I want to stay here, on deck. It's so..." She lifted her head to the breeze blowing up the Hudson, smelling of the sea. It was marvelous. But, live on a boat? The city skyline soared right beside them, almost on top of them. It was insane. Unpredictable. Extraordinary.

Kit knew her so well. And he loved her all the same. He'd do anything for her.

Couldn't she be as selfless? What good was a life without risk?

She'd thought she'd been adventurous, but she was only reckless because she kept nothing that mattered. With Kit, she would have to find the courage to be different.

He was holding up his glass of champagne, watching her and waiting.

The *tink* of her glass touching his was as clear as a bell. "I want to be eloquent and meaningful," she said, swallowing an icy mouthful of champagne to keep her voice from breaking. "I want so much..." She heard herself, and shook her head. "But that's not right. You bring me to this boat, you give me this beautiful gift and I'm going to think about myself? Uh-uh. No way."

She reached up to touch Kit's face. "I'm going to give you what you need, if I can."

They touched lips, foreheads. "But all I want is you," Kit said softly.

Sabrina smiled, kissing him. She was what he wanted, yes. But what he *needed*—well, that would come. They would negotiate, make compromises. It might take some time for her to figure out the boundaries of a new life, but she'd try, because always in her heart would be the knowledge that she loved Kit and he loved her. Their relationship would be like chocolate—fluid at times, solid at others, but never less than sweet and rich and good.

"You have me," she said between tender kisses. "In an apartment or on a boat, slaving over a hot stove, even floating adrift on a life raft—I'm yours."

"And I'm yours. So is this." He reached into his pocket.

She was almost afraid to look, even though she knew, she knew—

It was the velvet ring box.

"How did you...?"

"I overheard you mention a ring. Mackenzie told me about it when I went and asked her while you were busy planning the luncheon."

"But the ring's not really mine. Not anymore." She'd rather have Kit than a diamond anyway.

"Yes, it is." He opened the box, lifted out the ring and reached for her hand. "I know you gave it to Mackenzie for safekeeping, but she passed it on to me. She said that if I could actually get you to accept my proposal, you had to have the ring to seal the deal."

Sabrina sniffed. "I love this ring. It's not at all stylish, and it's not even very valuable because the diamond has a flaw. But it was always the lone remaining symbol I clung to, like my one last chance for love."

"One chance is all we need." Kit slipped the diamond onto her finger. "I promise, *chérie*, we're going to be very happy. Happy forever."

She hesitated, waiting for the cynical part of her that would point out that no one was happy all the time, but it wasn't there. Yet she wasn't transformed—she was elevated. She was *hopeful*.

But Kit wasn't finished. He produced a truffle, holding it up to her mouth between thumb and forefinger. "The secret ingredient," he said. "Chock-full of happy chemicals."

Sabrina didn't need chocolate to give her bliss, but she took the truffle anyway, biting it in half and inserting one of the pieces between Kit's lips. He accepted it eagerly, scraping his teeth and tongue across her finger, then sweeping her up in a kiss that melted, blended, sweetened and strengthened, swirling with chocolate and champagne and a love so pure and rich it had no price.

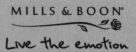

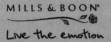

Next month don't miss –

CLAIMING HIS MISTRESS

*It's a convenient affair and strictly business.
It's a game they're both willing to play. But
what will happen when business by day turns
into passion by night…?*

On sale 6th February 2004

*Available at most branches of WHSmith, Tesco, Martins,
Borders, Eason, Sainsbury's and all good paperback bookshops.*

0104/05

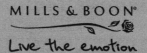

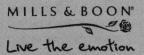

MILLS & BOON®

Live the emotion

Medical Romance™

THE DOCTOR'S FAMILY SECRET *by Joanna Neil*

When new A&E consultant Nick Hilliard sweeps in, full of ideas for change, Dr Laura Brett is torn between her attraction for this man and her concern for the department. But Nick becomes a rock for Laura – his support is unconditional. And then his ambitious plans start to affect her father, and her loyalties are divided...

A SURGEON FOR KATE *by Janet Ferguson*

Surgeon Lucas Brown may be the heart-throb of Seftonbridge General, but nurse Kate Maybury is staying well clear. A new relationship is the last thing on her agenda. But the sexual tension is crackling between them, and Kate knows she faces a struggle to hold on to her heart...

THE CONSULTANT'S TEMPTATION
by Emily Forbes

Gorgeous consultant Will MacLeod couldn't believe his luck when his new registrar, Alice Ferguson, turned out to be talented *and* beautiful. But he refused to endanger her promising career by indulging their chemistry. However, Alice was not going to let Will's scruples stand in the way of the love of a lifetime.

On sale 6th February 2004

Available at most branches of WHSmith, Tesco, Martins, Borders, Eason, Sainsbury's and all good paperback bookshops.

0104/03b

2 FREE

books and a surprise gift!

We would like to take this opportunity to thank you for reading this Mills & Boon® book by offering you the chance to take TWO more specially selected titles from the Sensual Romance™ series absolutely FREE! We're also making this offer to introduce you to the benefits of the Reader Service™—

> ★ FREE home delivery
> ★ FREE gifts and competitions
> ★ FREE monthly Newsletter
> ★ Exclusive Reader Service offers
> ★ Books available before they're in the shops

Accepting these FREE books and gift places you under no obligation to buy, you may cancel at any time, even after receiving your free shipment. Simply complete your details below and return the entire page to the address below. *You don't even need a stamp!*

YES! Please send me 2 free Sensual Romance books and a surprise gift. I understand that unless you hear from me, I will receive 4 superb new titles every month for just £2.60 each, postage and packing free. I am under no obligation to purchase any books and may cancel my subscription at any time. The free books and gift will be mine to keep in any case.

T4ZED

Ms/Mrs/Miss/Mr ....Initials...............................
BLOCK CAPITALS PLEASE

Surname ....

Address ....

....

....Postcode...............................

Send this whole page to:
UK: FREEPOST CN81, Croydon, CR9 3WZ
EIRE: PO Box 4546, Kilcock, County Kildare (stamp required)